Without the both trigger D0444561 d

. . . and was splattered by ichor of the exploding dog-thing.

Then he ran, throwing the spent shotgun aside as he fled. The ground erupted beneath the jeep. The armor-headed snake-thing had been waiting for him. Mike threw his arm over his face and screamed.

His cries were drowned out by the sound of a gauss rifle on full auto. Then a round found the remaining fuel in the jeep, and the entire vehicle went up, taking the serpent-thing with it.

There was a sound behind him. A large, thankfully human figure blocked the sunlight. Broad-shouldered, and packing a heavy slugthrower from a belt holster worn low on his hip.

As his vision cleared, Mike realized the figure wasn't in marine uniform. His pants were buckskin leather, well-worn and rough. A lightweight combat vest pegged him as some kind of military. So did the gauss rifle he was packing.

"You all right, son?" said the silhouette.

"Fine. Alive," Mike gasped. "You're not a marine."

The figure spat into the dust. "Not a marine? I guess I'll take that as a compliment. I'm the local law in these parts—Marshal Jim Raynor."

STARCRAFT®

LIBERTY'S CRUSADE

JEFF GRUBB

POCKET BOOKS
New York   London   Toronto   Sydney

This book is a work of fiction. Names, characters, places, and incidents are products of the author's imagination or are used fictitiously. Any resemblance to actual events or locales or persons, living or dead, is entirely coincidental.

An *Original* Publication of POCKET BOOKS

POCKET BOOKS, a division of Simon & Schuster, Inc.
1230 Avenue of the Americas, New York, NY 10020

ISBN: 0-671-04148-7

First Pocket Books printing March 2001

12 11 10 9 8 7

POCKET and colophon are registered trademarks of Simon & Schuster, Inc.

For information regarding special discounts for bulk purchases, please contact Simon & Schuster Special Sales at 1-800-456-6798 or business@simonandschuster.com

Cover illustration by Justin Thavirat

Printed in the U.S.A.

Dedicated to the fans of *StarCraft*, in particular my co-workers who have spent countless man-hours perfecting the zergling swarm assault.

ACKNOWLEDGMENTS

This novel is set in the heart of the *StarCraft* universe, which would not exist without the hard work of the talented designers, artists, and programmers at Blizzard Entertainment.

LIBERTY'S
CRUSADE

ANTEBELLUM

THE MAN IN THE TATTERED COAT STANDS IN A room of shadows, bathed in light. No, that is wrong: the figure is not illuminated by the light, but rather is light incarnate, light folded and curved in on itself in a holographic replica of its originator. The man speaks to the dimly lit room, unknowing and uncaring if there is anyone present beyond the limits of his own radiance. Phantom smoke, equally luminous, snakes up from the cigarette in his left hand.

He is a shard of the past, a bit of what had gone before, frozen in light, playing to an unseen audience.

"You know me," says the shining figure, pausing to take a drag on his coffin nail. "You've seen my face on the Universe News Network, and you've read the reports under my byline. Some of those were even written by me. Some others, well, let's say I have talented editors." The light-starred figure gives a tired, almost amused shrug.

The recording presents him as a small mannequin,

but he looks as if in real life he would be of normal height and proportions, if a little lanky. His shoulders slope slightly from exhaustion or age. His dirty-blond hair is spattered with lighter striations of gray and is swept back in a ponytail to hide an obvious bald spot. His face is worn, a bit craggier than would be permitted for a traditional newscast, but still recognizable. It remains a famous face, a comfortable face, a well-known face across human space, even in these later war-torn days.

But it is his eyes that demand attention. They are deep-set, and even in the recording seem to reach out. It is the eyes that create the illusion that the shining figure can truly see his audience, and see them to the core of their beings. That has always been his talent, connecting with his audience even when he was light-years away.

The figure takes another pull on his cancer stick, and his head is bathed in a holy nimbus of smoke. "You may have heard the official reports of the fall of the Confederacy of Man and of the glorious rise of the empire called the Terran Dominion. And you may have listened to the stories of the coming of the aliens, the hordes of Zerg and the inhuman, ethereal Protoss. Of the battles of the Sara system and the fall of Tarsonis itself. You've heard the reports. As I said before, some of those reports had my name on them. Parts of them are even true."

In the darkness beyond the light someone shifts uneasily, unseen. The holographic projector lets out only stray bits of light, rogue photons, but the audience remains for the moment a mystery. Somewhere behind the darkness-shrouded audience there is the sound of dripping water.

"You read my words, then, and believed them. I'm here to tell you, in those broadcasts, that most of them were grade-A cow patties, massaged by the powers that be into more suitable and palatable forms. Lies were told, both small and large, lies that have led us in part to our present sorry situation. A situation that is not going to improve unless we start talking about what really happened. What happened on Chau Sara and Mar Sara and Antiga Prime and Tarsonis itself. What happened to me and some friends of mine, and some enemies as well."

The figure pauses, drawing itself up to its full height. It looks around, its sightless eyes sweeping the darkened room. It looks into the core of its audience's soul.

"I'm Michael Daniel Liberty. I'm a reporter. Call this my most important, perhaps final, report. Call this my manifesto. Call it what you will. I'm just here to tell you what really happened. I'm here to set the record straight. I'm here to tell you the truth."

CHAPTER 1

THE PRESS GANG

Before the war, things were different. Hell, back then, we were just making our daily living, doing our jobs, drawing our paychecks, and stabbing our fellow men and women in the back. We had no idea how bad things would get. We were fat and happy like maggots on a dead animal. There was enough sporadic violence—rebellions and revolutions and balky colonial governments—to keep the military going, but not enough to really threaten the lifestyles we had grown accustomed to. We were, in retrospect, fat and sassy.

And if a real war broke out, well, it was the military's worry. The marines' worry. Not ours.

—THE LIBERTY MANIFESTO

THE CITY SPRAWLED BENEATH MIKE'S FEET LIKE an overturned bucket of jade cockroaches. From the dizzying height of Handy Anderson's office, he could almost see the horizon between the taller buildings. The city reached that far, forming a jagged, spiked tear along the edge of the world.

The city of Tarsonis, on the planet Tarsonis. The most important city on the most important planet of the Confederacy of Man. The city so great they named it twice. The city so large its suburbs had greater populations than some planets. A shining beacon of civilization, keeper of the memories of an Earth now lost to history, myth, and earlier generations.

A sleeping dragon. And Michael Liberty could not resist twisting its tail.

"Come back from the edge there, Mickey," said Anderson. The editor-in-chief was firmly ensconced at his desk, a desk as far away from the panoramic view as possible.

Michael Liberty liked to think there was a note of concern in his boss's voice.

"Don't worry," said Mike. "I'm not thinking of jumping." He suppressed a smile.

Mike and the rest of the newsroom knew that the editor-in-chief was acrophobic but could not bear to surrender his stratospheric office view. So on the rare occasions when Liberty was summoned into his boss's office, he always stood near the window. Most of the time he and the other drudges and news hacks worked way down on the fourth floor or in the broadcast booths in the building's basement.

"Jumping I'm not worried about," said Anderson. "Jumping I can handle. Jumping would solve a lot of my problems and give me a lead for tomorrow's edition. I'm more worried about some sniper taking you out from another building."

Liberty turned toward his boss. "Bloodstains that hard to get out of the carpet?"

"Part of it," said Anderson, smiling. "It's also a bitch to replace the glass."

Liberty look one last look at the traffic crawling far below and returned to the overstuffed chairs facing the desk. Anderson tried to be nonchalant, but Mike noted that the editor let out a long, slow breath as Mike moved away from the window.

Michael Liberty settled himself into one of Anderson's chairs. The chairs were designed to look like normal furniture, but they were stuffed so that they sank an extra inch or two when someone sat down. This made the balding editor-in-chief with his comically oversized eyebrows look more imposing. Mike knew the trick, was not impressed, and set his feet up on the desk.

"So what's the beef?" the reporter asked.

"Have a cigar, Mickey?" Anderson motioned with an open palm toward a teak humidor.

Mike hated being called Mickey. He touched his empty shirt pocket, where he normally stashed a pack of cigarettes. "I'm on the wagon. Trying to cut down."

"They're from beyond the Jaandaran embargo," said Anderson temptingly. "Rolled on the thighs of cinnamon-shaded maidens."

Mike held up both hands and smiled broadly. Everyone knew that Anderson was too cheap to get anything beyond the standard *el ropos* manufactured in some bootleg basement. But the smile was intended to reassure.

"What's the beef?" Mike repeated.

"You've really done it this time," said Anderson, sighing. "Your series on the construction kickbacks on the new Municipal Hall."

"Good stuff. The series should rattle a few cages."

"They've already been rattled," replied Anderson, his chin sinking down to touch his chest. This was known as the bearer-of-bad-news position. It was something that Anderson had learned at some management course but that made him look like a mating ledge-pigeon.

Crap, thought Mike. *He's going to spike the series.*

As if reading his thoughts, Anderson said, "Don't worry, we're going to run the rest of the series. It's solid reporting, well-documented, and best of all, it's true. But you have to know you've made a few people very uncomfortable."

Mike mentally ran through the series. It had been one of his better ones, a classic involving a petty offender who was caught in the wrong place (a public park) at the wrong time (way after midnight) with the wrong thing (mildly radioactive construction waste from the Municipal Hall project). Said offender was more than willing to pass on the name of the man who sent him on this late-night escapade. That individual was in turn willing to tell Mike about some other interesting matters involving the new hall, and so forth, until Mike had, instead of a single story, a whole series about a huge network of graft and corruption that the Universe

Network News audience ate up with their collective spoons.

Mike mentally ran through the ward heelers, low-level thugs, and members of the Tarsonis City Council that he had skewered in print, discarding each in turn as a suspect. Any of those august individuals might want to take a shot at him, but such a threat wasn't enough to make Handy Anderson nervous.

The editor-in-chief saw Mike's blank expression and added, "You've made a few powerful, *venerable* people very uncomfortable."

Mike's left eyebrow rose. Anderson was talking about one of the ruling Families, the power behind the Confederacy for most of its existence, since those early days when the first colony ships (hell, prison ships) landed and/or crashed on various planets in the sector. Somewhere in his reporting, he had nailed somebody with pull, or perhaps somebody close enough to one of the Families to make the old venerables nervous.

Mike resolved to go back over his notes and see what kind of linkages he could make. Perhaps a distaff cousin to one of the Old Families, or a black sheep, or maybe even a direct kickback. God knew that the Old Families ran things from behind the scenes since the year naught. If he could nail one of them . . .

Mike wondered if he was visibly salivating at the prospect.

In the meantime Handy Anderson had risen from his seat and strolled around the side of his desk, perching on the corner nearest Mike. (Another move directly out of the management lectures, Mike realized. Hell, Anderson had assigned him to cover those lectures once.) "Mike, I want you to know you're on dangerous ground here."

Oh God, he called me Mike, thought Liberty. *Next he'll be looking plaintively out the window as if lost in thought, wrestling with a momentous decision.*

He said, "I'm used to dangerous ground, boss."

"I know, I know. I just worry about those around you. Your sources. Your friends. Your co-workers . . ."

"Not to mention my superiors."

". . . all of whom would be heartbroken if something horrible happened to you."

"Particularly if they were standing nearby when it happened," added the reporter.

Anderson shrugged and stared plaintively out the full-length window. Mike realized that whatever Anderson was afraid of, it was worse than his fear of heights. And this was a man who, if office rumor was correct (and it was), kept a locked room in the subbasement that contained dirt on most of the celebrities and important citizens of the city.

The pause dragged beyond a moment into a minute. Finally Mike broke. He gave a polite cough and said, "So you have an idea how to handle this 'dangerous ground'?"

Handy Anderson nodded slowly. "I want to print the series. It's good work."

"But you don't want me anywhere in the immediate vicinity when the next part of that story hits the street."

"I'm thinking of your own safety, Mickey, it's . . ."

"Dangerous ground," finished Mike. "I heard. Here be dragons. Perhaps it would be time for an extended vacation? Maybe a cabin in the mountains?"

"I was thinking more of a special assignment."

Of course, thought Mike. *That way I won't have the chance to figure out whose tail I've inadvertently twisted. And give those involved time to cover their tracks.*

"Another part of the Universe News Network empire?" Mike said with a broad smile, at the same time wondering what godforsaken colony world he would be doing agricultural reports from.

"More of a roving reporter," teased Anderson.

"How roving?" Mike's smile suddenly became flinty and brittle. "Will I need shots for off-planet?"

"Better than getting shot for being on-planet. Sorry, bad joke. The answer is yes, I'm thinking definitely off-planet."

"Come on, spill. Which hellhole do you want to hide me in?"

"I was thinking of the Confederate Marines. As a military reporter, of course."

"What!"

"It would be a temporary posting, of course," continued the editor.

"Are you out of your *mind?*"

"Sort of 'our fighting men in space,' battling against the various forces of rebellion that threaten our great

Confederacy. There are rumors that Arcturus Mengsk is rallying more support in the Fringe Worlds. Could turn really hot at any moment."

"The marines?" sputtered Mike. "The Confederate Marines are the biggest collection of criminals in the known universe, outside of the Tarsonis City Council."

"Mike, please. Everyone has *some* criminal blood in them. Hell, all the planets of the Confederacy were settled by exiled convicts."

"Yeah, but most people like to think we grew out of that. The marines still make that one of their basic recruiting requirements. Hell, do you know how many of them have been brain-panned?"

"Neurally Resocialized," corrected Anderson. "No more than fifty percent per unit these days, I understand. Less in some places. And the resocialization is more often done with noninvasive procedures. You probably won't notice."

"Yeah, and they pump them so full of stimpacks they'd kill their own grandpas on the right command."

"Exactly the sort of common misconception that your work can counter," said Anderson, both eyebrows raised in practiced sincerity.

"Look, most of the politicos I've met are naturally nuts. The marines are nuts and *then* they started messing with their heads. No. The marines are not an option."

"It'd make for some good stories. You'd probably get some good contacts."

"No."

"Reporters with experience with the military get perks," said the editor-in-chief. "You get a green tag on your file, and that carries weight with the more venerable families of Tarsonis. In some cases even for-giveness."

"Sorry. Not interested."

"I'll give you your own column."

A pause. Finally Mike said, "How big a column?"

"Full column-page print, or five minutes stand-up for the broadcast. Under your byline, of course."

"Regular?"

"You file, I'll fill."

Another pause. "A raise with that?"

Anderson named a figure, and Mike nodded.

"That's impressive," he said.

"Not chump change," agreed the editor-in-chief.

"I'm a little old to be planet-hopping."

"There's no real danger. And if something does flare up, there's combat pay. Automatic."

"Fifty percent brain-panned?" Mike asked.

"If that."

Another pause. Then Mike said, "Well, it sounds like a challenge."

"And you're just the man for a challenge."

"And it can't be worse than covering the Tarsonis City Council," Mike mused, feeling himself sliding down the slippery slope to acceptance.

"My thoughts exactly," his editor agreed.

"And if it would help the network . . ." Yep, Mike

thought, he was on the edge, poised to pitch over into the void.

"You would be a shining light to us all," said Anderson. "A well-paid, shining light. Wave the flag a little, get some personal stories, ride around in a battlecruiser, play some cards. Don't worry about us back here at the office."

"Cush posting?"

"Cushiest. I've got some pull, you know. Was an old green-tag myself. Three months work, tops. A lifetime of rewards."

There was a final pause, a chasm as deep as the concrete canyon that yawned beyond the window.

"All right," said Mike, "I'll do it."

"Wonderful!" Anderson reached for the humidor, then caught himself and instead offered Mike his hand. "You won't regret it."

"Why do I feel that I already do?" Michael Liberty asked in a small voice as the editor's meaty, sweaty hand ensnared his own.

CHAPTER 2

THE CUSH POSTING

Service in the military, for those of you unfortunate enough never to have experienced it firsthand, consists of long periods of boredom broken by mind-shredding threats to one's life and sanity. From what I can gather from the old tapes, it's always been like that. The best soldiers are those who can wake suddenly, react instantly, and aim precisely.

Unfortunately, none of those traits are shared by the military intelligence that controls those soldiers.

—The Liberty Manifesto

"MR. LIBERTY?" SAID THE PERKY MURDERESS AT THE hatchway. "The captain would like a word with you."

Michael Liberty, UNN reporter assigned to the elite Alpha Squadron of the Confederate Marines, propped open one eye and found her, all smiles, standing next to his bunk. An all-night card game had just adjourned, and he was sure the young marine lieutenant had waited until he had lain down before barging into his quarters.

The reporter let out a deep sigh and said, "Does Colonel Duke expect me immediately?"

"No, sir," said the murderess, shaking her head for effect. "He said you should come at your leisure."

"Right," said Mike, swinging his legs over the edge of his bunk and shaking the temptation of sleep from his brain. For Colonel Duke, "at your leisure" usually meant "within the next ten minutes, dammit." Mike reached for his cigarettes, and only when his hand had dipped into the empty shirt pocket did he remember he had given them up.

"Filthy habit anyway," he muttered to himself. To the marine lieutenant he said "Need a shower. Coffee would be good, too."

Lieutenant Emily Jameson Swallow, Liberty's personal assistant, liaison, minder, and spy for her military superiors, waited only long enough to determine that Mike was serious about getting up, then beetled off to the galley. Mike yawned, figured he must have had all of five minutes' sleep, stripped, and padded off to the sonic cleanser.

The sonic cleanser was a military model, of course. This meant it was similar in construction to those high-pressure jets that blasted the meat off the bones at slaughterhouses. In the past three months Mike had gotten used to it.

In the past three months Michael Liberty had gotten used to a lot of things.

Handy Anderson had been true to his word. The posting was posh, or at least as posh as a military assignment could be. The *Norad II* was a capital ship, one of the *Behemoth*-class, all neosteel and laser turrets, as befitted the most legendary of Confederate military units, the Alpha Squadron.

Alpha Squadron's primary mission was hunting rebels, particularly the Sons of Korhal, a revolutionary group under the bloodthirsty terrorist Arcturus Mengsk. Unfortunately, the Sons were never where they were supposed to be, and the *Norad II* and her prized crew spent a lot of time showing the flag (a blue diagonal cross filled with white stars against a red background, the memory of a legend of Old Earth) and keeping the local colonial governments in line.

As a result, Mike's biggest challenge so far had been dealing with boredom and finding enough to write about to justify his column. The flag-waving propaganda came easy for the first few stories, but when there was a deficit of real action or achievement, Mike had to reach. A piece on Colonel Edmund Duke, of course. Some human-interest stuff on the well-oiled crew. A bit about the travails of the neurally resocialized that Anderson scotched (out of common decency, Handy explained). Local color on the various planets. Just enough to remind everyone (Handy Anderson in particular) that he was still alive and expected regular payments to his account.

And then there was a long two-parter about the wonders of the *Behemoth*-class battlecruisers, a story that was decimated by military censors to a mere few paragraphs. Military secrets, it was explained.

Like the Sons of Korhal don't know what we have already, thought Mike as he slipped into his shorts and looked for a less rumpled shirt and pants. Hanging in his locker was a new traveling coat, a going-away present from the guys in the newsroom. It was a long duster that made him look like a denizen of the Old West, but the crew apparently felt that if Mike was going out to the interplanetary sticks, he might as well look the part.

He slipped into some nondescript pants. Almost on cue, Swallow reappeared with a pot of java and a mug. She poured as Mike buttoned up his shirt.

The brew was military style "A"—freshly made and scalding, suitable for pouring down on peasants attacking the family castle. The coffee was another thing he had gotten used to.

Of course, he had also gotten used to three squares, sufficient time to write his columns, and a flexible amount of privacy. As well as an ever-changing group of poker partners, all of whom were young, had no place to spend their paychecks, and could not bluff if their lives depended on it.

He had even gotten used to Lieutenant Swallow, though her habitual positive attitude bothered him at first. He had expected some sort of minder, of course, some military attaché who would hang over his shoulder as he wrote and make sure he didn't do anything stupid like drop his pen into the warp coils. But Lieutenant Emily Swallow was like something out of a training film. A particularly cheery training film, the type you show Mom and Dad before shipping their sons and daughters off to extended duty five star systems away. Hell, Lieutenant Emily Swallow looked like she *wrote* that type of training film.

Small, petite, and always smiling, she seemed to take every request from Mike seriously, even if they both knew that there was a snowball's chance that it would be approved. She had no vices, except for the occasional cigarette, accepted with a smile and a guilty shrug. Further, when he hit her up for her own story, she demurred. Most of the crew were stoked up, talking about their lives back home, but Lieutenant Swallow instead just stopped smiling and ran her hand back along the side of her face, as if brushing away long hair that was no longer there.

That was when Mike noticed the small divots behind her ear, the marks of the noninvasive neural resocialization that Anderson had mentioned. Yeah, she had been brain-panned, and good. No one could be that perky without an electrochemical lobotomy.

Mike didn't bring up the subject again, but instead bribed one of the computer techs for some time with the personnel files (this cost him his two emergency packs of smokes, but by that time he was through the worst of the cravings, and the coffin nails were better used in trade than consumption). He found out that before she had involuntarily joined the marines, young Emily Swallow had the interesting hobby of attracting young men in bars, taking them to her home, tying them up, and flaying the skin and meat from their bones with a fillet knife.

Most men would be disconcerted by this news, but Michael Liberty found it reassuring. The murderess of ten young men on Halcyon was much more understandable than the smiling, gung-ho woman who looked like someone from a recruiting poster. Now, following her through the corridors of the *Norad II* to the bridge, Mike wondered how Lieutenant Swallow felt about her medical incarceration and involuntary transformation. He decided that she just didn't dwell on it, and given her original nature, Mike decided not to press the issue.

For a huge ship, the *Norad II* had narrow passageways, built almost as an afterthought after all the landing bays, wardrooms, weapons systems, galleys, computers, and other necessities had been piled in. In the hallways oncoming traffic had to press against walls to pass. Mike noticed large arrows painted on the floor, which Lieutenant Swallow noted were for times when the ship was on alert and soldiers were in full battle armor. Mike realized that the gangways would have been made even narrower had they not been expected to accommodate men in powered combat suits.

They passed several large bays where technicians were already pulling out wiring and cables. The scuttlebutt was that the *Norad II* was due for an overhaul, including an upgrade with the Yamato cannon. Given the number of laser batteries, *Wraith*-class space fighters, and even the rumored nuclear arms carried onboard, the huge spine-mounted cannon would be icing on the cake.

In fact, this was what Mike expected Colonel Duke to tell him—that the *Norad II* was going into dry dock for repairs, and he, Michael Liberty, would be on the next shuttle back to Tarsonis. That would make dealing with the old fossil almost worthwhile.

He revised his opinion when they stepped onto the bridge, and Duke scowled at him. Mind you, Duke never looked particularly pleased to see a member of the press, but this was the deepest and most hostile scowl that Mike had seen yet.

"Mr. Liberty, reporting as requested, sir," said Lieutenant Swallow with a salute as sharp as that in any recruiting video.

The colonel, decked out in his command brown uniform, said nothing but pointed a stubby finger toward his ready room. Lieutenant Swallow led him there, then abandoned him for whatever tasks she did when she wasn't keeping tabs on him. Probably, Mike mused, something involving skinning puppies.

Mike's initial concern grew deeper when he recognized the humanoid shape now hanging from a wall-mounted frame in the ready room. It was a powered combat suit, not one of the standard-issue CMC-300s but a command suit, fitted with its own portable comm system. Colonel Duke's suit, now shined and greased and ready for the great man to step into it.

Mike was less sure now that they were going in for that Yamato refit. Most of the marines kept their armor handy, and drills were as common as meals. Liberty managed to avoid that duty, as he was considered a "soft target" and wasn't cleared for the heavier suits. It was, however, amusing to see the rookies staggering around the narrow passages in full combat armor.

But for the colonel's suit to be here, newly polished and ready, boded very ill indeed.

The suit itself was massive, hunched forward on the hanger under its own weight. In that way, it seemed to Michael Liberty, the empty suit fit its owner well. Colonel Duke reminded Mike of the great apes of Old Earth, the ones that climbed buildings and swatted down primitive aircraft. Gorillas. Duke was an old silverback, the pointy-headed leader of his tribe, and just the way he leaned forward inspired fear in his subordinates.

Mike knew that Duke was from one of the Old Families, the original leaders of the Koprulu Sector colonies. But he must have done something wrong along the way: Edmund Duke was obviously long overdue for his general's stars. Mike wondered what nasty incident stood in the way of his promotion, and surmised that it was loud, messy, and deeply buried in the Confederate military files. He wondered what type of pull it would take to get that information out, and if Handy Anderson had it in his not-so-secret vault.

The door slid open and Colonel Duke strode in like a *Goliath*-style armored walker scattering infantry units before it. His scowl was even deeper than earlier. He held down a hand to indicate that Mike shouldn't rise (Mike had had no intention of doing so), circled his wide desk, and sat down. He rested his elbows on the polished obsidian desktop and templed his fingers in front of him.

"I trust, Liberty, you have had an enjoyable time with us?" he asked. He had the old, faint drawl that marked the elder Families of the Confederacy.

Mike, who had not expected small talk, managed to stammer out a general affirmative.

"I am afraid it will not last," said the colonel. "Our original orders were to be relieved by the *Theodore G. Bilbo*, and to put in for a retrofit within two weeks. Events have now overtaken us."

Mike said nothing. He had been in enough briefings over the years, even on a civilian level, to know not to interrupt until he had something worth interrupting for.

"We are rerouting our course to the Sara system. I'm afraid it's in the boonies, on the butt end of nowhere. The Confederacy has two colony worlds there, Mar Sara and Chau Sara. This is an extended patrol over and above our initial mission parameters."

Mike just nodded. The colonel was creeping up on the subject, acting like a dog with a chicken bone in its throat—something he had a hard time swallowing and a worse time coughing back up. Mike waited.

"I must remind you that as a member of the press assigned to the Alpha Squadron, you are limited under the Confederate military code in regard to what your duties are and how you perform them."

"Yes, sir," said Mike, sternly enough to give the impression that he gave a rat's ass about the Confederate military code.

"And that this extends to your current assignment as well as to future references to events that occur during your posting here." Duke nodded his pointed head, clearly demanding a response.

"Yes, sir." Mike separated the words clearly to underscore his comprehension.

Another pause, during which Mike could feel the throbbing of the ship around him. Yes, the *Norad II* was vibrating at a different pitch now, a bit higher, more intense, a bit more frantic. Men and women were preparing the ship for subwarp. And perhaps for combat?

Mike suddenly wondered about the wisdom of skipping those combat suit drills.

Colonel Edmund Duke, the dog with the chicken bone in his throat, said, "You know our histories."

It was more of a statement than a question. Mike blinked, suddenly unsure how to respond. He settled for "Sir?"

"How we came to the sector and settled it. Took it for our own," prompted the colonel.

"Aboard the sleeper ships, the supercarriers," Mike said, pulling up the lessons of childhood. "The *Nagglfar*, the *Argo*, the *Sarengo*, and the *Reagan*. The crews of prisoners and outcasts of Old Earth, crashing onto a scattering of habitable worlds."

"And they found three such worlds, right off the bat.

And a double-handful nearby that were terrestrial or close enough for army work. But they found no life."

"Begging the colonel's pardon, but there was extensive native life on all three original planets. Plus, most of the colonies and Fringe Worlds have their own ecosystems. Terraforming often, but not always, eradicates native life-forms."

The colonel waved off the comment. "But nothing smarter than your standard watchdog. Some big insects they domesticated on Umoja, and a lot of stuff that was burned when the world was settled and put under the plow. But nothing *smart*."

Mike nodded. "Intelligent life has always been one of the mysteries of the universe. We have found world after world, but nothing to indicate that there is something else out there as smart as we are."

"Until now," said the colonel. "And you will be the first network reporter on the scene."

Mike warmed a bit to the subject. "There have been numerous mysterious formations on many planets that indicate there might have been sentient life at one time. In addition, there are space-haulers' tales of mysterious lights and foo-fighters."

"These aren't lights in the sky or old ruins. This is living proof of ET activity. That we are not alone out here."

Duke let that sink in, and a smirk tugged at the side of his mouth. It did not improve his appearance in the least. Somewhere within the ship a switch closed, and the monstrous engines began to hum.

Mike stroked his chin and asked, "What do we know so far? Has there been an envoy, a representative? Or was this a chance discovery? Did we find a colony, or was there a direct embassy?"

The colonel let out a gruff chortle. "Mr. Liberty, let me make myself quite clear. We have made contact with another alien civilization. This contact consisted of them vaporizing the colony of Chau Sara. They burned it to the ground, and then burned the ground beneath it. We're going there now, but we don't know if the hostiles are still present.

"And you will be the first network reporter on the scene," repeated the colonel. "Congratulations, son."

Mike didn't feel very good about this particular honor.

CHAPTER 3

THE SARA SYSTEM

The first contact with another sentient race, and they blow up a planet. Helluva calling card.

Now, blowing up a planet is nothing new. Christ, we humans did it ourselves not too long ago.

There was a revolt on the planet Korhal IV. The inhabitants didn't care much for the graft and corruption that was part and parcel of the Confederacy. They tried to rebel. At first the Confederacy tried a soft approach: they took out the rebellion's leaders with assassins, ghost-troopers with personal cloaking devices. Unsurprisingly, this approach just made the people of Korhal angrier and more rebellious. So the Confederacy took a harder line.

We nuked Korhal IV from orbit.

Apocalypse-class missiles. About a thousand of them. Some green-tagged idiot on Tarsonis pressed a button, and 35 million people became nothing more than vapor and their homes nothing more than a memory.

Naturally, there were official justifications thereafter about the evil, menacing nature of Korhal, and how they were planning to do it to us if they got even the slightest chance. It was unfortunate that the proof of this accusation was located on a planet covered by blackened glass.

I think that's what really scared the military about the vaporization of Chau Sara: that there was something else out there that was just as crazy as we were.

And they were better at it than we were.

—THE LIBERTY MANIFESTO

MIKE TOOK ADVANTAGE OF THE TIME THE SHIP was in subwarp to pore through the open computer archives on the Sara system. It was a fairly typical Fringe system, the ragged leading edge of the Confederacy's ever-increasing sphere of power.

The system had been found by a prospector before the Guild Wars, glommed onto by the Confederacy when it eclipsed that budding rival in space, and was (according to the ship's archives) the home of a growing pair of colony worlds. The only thing that made the Sara system different from about a dozen other similar worlds was that there were two worlds in its habitable band instead of just one.

Chau Sara was the smaller and more outlying of the worlds, and had the larger colony. It had been settled, in Confederate tradition, as a penal colony, and a lot of its (now former) inhabitants had still been serving hard time. Mar Sara had a more eclectic mix of former prospectors and soldiers, along with a couple of religious types that didn't agree with the Tarsonian limits of tolerance for other faiths. Both planets had rich potential for mineral exploitation, but of course the Confederacy had dibs on those resources. The locals would have to either work under Confederate contracts or flee to new Fringe Worlds.

Mike checked the current UNN reports. There was a small bit about a disruption of signals from the Sara system, but most of the broadcast was given over to the latest Sons of Korhal outrage (poison gas in a public plaza on Haji), and a multitrain monorail pileup on Moira.

Mike composed a brief blurb, summarizing his discussion with Colonel Duke and noting that he was under full military restrictions in future reporting. That meant that his report would be checked over before it left the ship and then again before it was broadcast. Handy Anderson would be simultaneously griping about military censorship and dancing around his office in joy for the scoop.

If I'm lucky, thought Mike, *he'll dance too close to that damned window of his.*

Mike prepared a second report, this one scrambled under cipher software and burned onto a minidisk. This one wasn't going anywhere, but if something happened to them, and their bodies were found, someone would know what was going on. It was a grim insurance policy.

He had just finished the second report when a large shadow blocked the light.

Mike looked up into the face of Lieutenant Swallow, now a foot taller and several hundred pounds heavier. She was decked out in a combat suit, her natural strength boosted by servos and mechanisms. An empty belt clip at her side would soon be filled with an 8-millimeter C-14 gauss rifle, an Impaler, for when she went into action.

Her visor was open, and she beamed an excited smile at him. She looked like a girl expecting her first prom dance.

"Sir? We'll be coming out of subwarp soon. The colonel wants you on the bridge, at the soonest possible moment." Then she was gone.

Meaning right damned now, thought Mike, and followed Swallow out of his quarters.

The passageways were no wider now, but with the bulky suits now in preponderance they had become one-way, with movement guided by huge arrows on the floor. At several crossings Swallow held up to let other crewmen pass in front of them, and Mike had the sudden feeling of being the only kindergartner in a sixth-grade class.

"I've got to get me one of those suits," he commented.

"I was unaware you were trained in the CMC powered combat suit, sir," said Swallow.

"I've read the manuals."

"That knowledge would be barely sufficient for your own protection in a crisis situation, sir. However, should something happen, it is my personal responsibility to make sure you get to safety."

"I'm filled with confidence." Mike smiled at Swallow's back, just in case she had a camera trained on him.

The ship gave a transdimensional shudder, and the engines shifted back from subwarp. They were in Sara's space.

The bridge was now bathed in red light, accented by the green monitors that lined the lower deck. Colonel Duke was decked out in his own battle armor. He looked like a gorilla at the court of King Arthur. A gorilla with a pointy head, wearing plate mail. He was surrounded by a small cluster of viewscreens, each with a different talking head feeding data to him.

"Mr. Liberty, reporting as requested, sir," said Swallow, managing another sharp salute, even in the heavy armor.

"Colonel," said Mike.

Duke did not look away from the main screen. He said simply, "We're nearing Chau Sara."

At first Mike thought the main screen was malfunctioning. They were approaching Chau Sara from the night side. The large disk of the outer Saran world was a messy, rainbow smear of light, like that found on oily water.

Then Mike realized that this *was* the surface of Chau Sara he was looking at. It glowed with rippling bands of colors, moored at a handful of locations by bright spikes of orange.

"What . . ." Mike blinked. "What did this?"

"First contact, Liberty," said the colonel. "First contact of the most extreme kind. How are the scans?"

One of the technicians reported, "I get no life readings. Most of the surface area has been liquefied and sterilized. This zone looks to be between twenty and fifty feet deep."

"The settlements?" Mike asked.

The technician continued, "The orange spikes appear to be magma breaches through the planetary mantle. They are located at the locations of the known settlements." A pause. "Plus at least a dozen other locations."

Mike looked at the swirling, deadly rainbow on the screen. The sun was cresting the horizon ahead of them, and the world looked no better in the sunlight. Only a few dark clouds, thin as crow feathers, dragged across the sunlight side.

"In addition, eighty percent of the atmosphere has been blown off in the attack," continued the technician.

"Any orbital presence?" asked Duke, an armor-plated monolith in their midst.

"Working," said the tech. Finally came the response, "Negative. Nothing of ours. Nothing of unknown origin either. There may be some fragments on a larger scan."

"Widen the scan," said Duke. "I want to know if there's anything out here. Ours or theirs."

"Working . . . Definite fragments. Likely ours. Would need a salvage team to confirm."

"Why did they do this?" Mike asked, but no one answered him. Techs in lighter-weight combat suits tapped displays with gauntleted hands, and the numerous heads on the screens all talked at once to Colonel Duke.

Finally Mike came up with a question he thought they could answer. "What did this? Nukes?"

The word seemed to break Duke from his steady stream of information. He looked at the reporter. "Atomic delivery systems leave blackened glass and burning forests. Even Korhal had some surviving pockets of clear terrain, for a while at least. Chau Sara has been burned down to the liquid core in places. This is much more deadly than even Apocalypse bombs."

"This"—Duke pointed at the screen—"is the work of an alien race, the Protoss. From what I'm being told, they warped in from nowhere, closer to the planet than we would ever attempt. Huge ships, and a lot of them. Caught a few transports and scavenger ships and blew them out of the sky. Then they unleashed whatever-it-was on the planet and sterilized it like a three-minute egg. Then they left again. Mar Sara's on the other side of the sun right now, and they're in a panic that they might be next."

"Protoss." Mike shook his head slightly, digesting the data. Something was wrong there. He looked at the tech's display, showing the deep radar holes punching down to the planet's magma.

"You have enough for your report, Mr. Liberty," Duke said. "We will remain on station in the event of other hostiles for the foreseeable future. You may mention in any report you file that we will be joined by the *Jackson V* and the *Huey Long* within days."

The tech reached for his ear, then said, "Sir, we have anomalous readings."

"Location?" snapped the colonel, turning away from Liberty.

"Zed-Two, Quadrant Five, one AU out. Numerous anomalies."

"Bearing?"

"Working." A pause, and then a defeated shrug crept into the tech's words. "Heading for Mar Sara, sir."

Duke nodded. "Prepare to intercept anomalous readings. Launch fighters when in range."

Mike spoke before he thought, "Are you crazy?"

Duke turned back to the reporter. "That was a rhetorical question, I hope, son."

"We're one ship."

"We're the only ship between them and Mar Sara. We will intercept."

Mike almost said, "Easy for you, you're in a hard-shelled battlesuit," but caught himself. Whatever could go through a planetary crust wouldn't be stopped by a few layers of combat armor.

Instead Mike took a deep breath and just gripped the railing, as if he were hoping that this might ease the eventual blow.

"Approaching visual," said the tech. "Putting on screen."

The main screen flickered to reveal a scattering of

fireflies against the night sky. They looked almost pretty against the darkness. Then Mike realized that there were hundreds of them, and that these were only the main ships. Smaller gnats danced around them.

"Are we within launching range for the Wraiths?" the colonel asked.

"Mark at two minutes," replied the tech.

"Launch as soon as possible."

Mike took a deep breath and wished that he had joined in the combat suit drills after all.

Even at long range, the Protoss ships had form and definition. The largest were huge cylindrical creations, similar in appearance to luminous zeppelins. They were surrounded by hungry moths, and Mike realized these had to be their fighters, their equivalents of the A-17 Wraiths that were now in the hangars, just waiting for them to close to within striking range. Other golden ships danced between the larger carriers, glimmering like small stars.

Then, as Mike watched, one of the great carriers seemed to dissolve. There was a flash of light, a soft glowing, and then it was gone. Another moment, and another flash, and another disappearance.

"Sir," said the technician. "Anomalous reading disappearing."

"Cloaking technology?" asked the colonel.

Despite himself, Mike said, "At this scale?"

"Working." A huge pause, as deep as a canyon. "Negative. It appears that they are surrounding themselves with some form of subwarp field. They are retreating."

As Mike watched, more of the ships began to flash and vanish. The great carriers and their brood of smaller ships, the lesser golden vessels, all vanished like fey spirits with the coming of dawn.

Fey spirits that can burn a planet down to its molten core, Mike reminded himself.

The colonel allowed himself a smile. "Good. They're afraid of us. Have all stations stand down, but remain alert for a trick."

Mike shook his head. "This makes no sense. They have the power to toast a planet. Why are they afraid of us?"

"Obvious," said the colonel. "They're spent. They don't have enough force to engage us."

"We're only one ship." Mike shook his head angrily. "There were dozens out there."

"They fear possible reinforcements."

"No, no. Something's going on here. It doesn't make human sense."

"We're not dealing with humans here," said Duke, scowling. "Look at their firepower."

"Exactly. These Protoss have superior numbers and firepower, and *we're* facing them down? Why *are* they here?"

"Mr. Liberty, that will be enough questions for the day." The scowl deepened, but Mike ignored the warning.

"No, something's not jake in all this. Look at the

damage reports." Mike pointed at one of the tech's monitors. "They cooked an entire planet, but some places deeper than others. Every major human city, yes, but look." Mike pointed at the wall of data. "There are strike zones on the other side of the planet, far away from any recorded human settlement. I know. I was just checking the archives."

"I said that will be *enough*, Mister. We have more to worry about with the Protoss than just how effective they are in choosing their targets."

Mike's face lit up as a connection was made deep in his brain. "And where did we get the name 'Protoss,' Colonel? Is that ours, or theirs?"

"Mister Liberty!" Color was creeping up the sides of Duke's face.

"And if it's their name for themselves, how come *we* know it? Didn't we have to know it in advance? Or did they send a warning before they attacked?" The reporter was raising his voice now, the way he would for a dissembling candidate in a precinct by-election.

"Lieutenant Swallow!" Duke bit off the command.

"Yes, sir?" Another perfect salute.

"Escort Mr. Liberty off the bridge! Now!"

Mike gripped the railing firmly with both hands. A ligatured arm wrapped in metal snaked around his waist. Mike was shouting now, "Dammit, Duke, you know more than you're telling. This stinks to high heaven!"

"I said now, Lieutenant!" Duke snarled.

"This way, sir," said Swallow, breaking Mike's hold and pulling the reporter off his feet. With her prize, she retreated for the lift.

Still shouting questions, Michael Liberty left the bridge. The last thing he heard before the doors slid shut was Colonel Duke ordering the opening of a comm line with the colonial magistrate of Mar Sara.

CHAPTER 4

DOWN ON MAR SARA

There's a period in any war between the first blow and the second. It's a quiet moment, an almost tranquil time, when the realization of what has happened is just sinking in and everyone feels they know what happens next. Some prepare to flee. Some prepare to hit back. But no one moves. Not yet.

It's a perfect moment, the time when the ball is at the highest point of the throw. The action has been taken, and for one frozen moment everything is moving, but everything is at rest.

Then there are those jackasses who can't leave such things alone. And the ball starts downward again, the second blow is thrown, and we plunge into the maelstrom.

—The Liberty Manifesto

MICHAEL LIBERTY WAS NOT ALLOWED OUT OF his quarters for the remainder of the action over Mar Sara. Lieutenant Swallow or one of her neurally resocialized comrades stood guard outside his quarters for the next two days. After that it was an escort to the dropship and a shuttle to beautiful Mar Sara itself.

Now, a day after that, he was in the press pool, fleecing the local reporters for most of their life savings while waiting for something that resembled a straight answer from the powers that be.

It was not forthcoming. The official debriefings were preshaped pellets of non-news that stressed the suddenness of the attack on Chau Sara, hailed Duke and the *Norad II* crew as heroes for standing up to the enemy, and claimed that only the everwatchful vigilance of the Confederacy could protect Mar Sara. The Protoss (still no idea where the name came from) were portrayed as cowards who folded at the first sign of a real fight. The delicate if impressive nature of their lightning-charged ships confirmed that notion: they fled because they were afraid to be hit.

That was the story, anyway, and the marines were sticking with it. In fact, if anyone in the press pool wandered too far from the official version, their reports suddenly started getting lost in transmission. That kept most of the locals in line. They were all issued passes with bar codes that were supposed to be presented upon demand. And, Mike knew, to keep tabs on their whereabouts.

All of the other newshounds knew Liberty's story from aboard the *Norad II*, but no one had yet tried to use any of the information in their own reports.

In the outside world, a planetary lockdown was in force. Officially a civilian protection measure (to quote the official press release), it was effectively a military overthrow of the local government. The locals were being herded into concentration points for supposedly easier evacuation. No mention was made of where the evacuating ships would come from, or even if there was a timetable for abandoning the planet. In the meantime, there were marine patrols on every corner, and those citizens who remained in the city were looking very, very nervous.

In the absence of anything reportable, the newshounds hung out at the large café in front of the Grand Hotel, played cards, waited for the next official news-like release, and speculated madly. Mike, bedecked in his duster, lounged with them, looking more like a native than any of the others.

"Man, I don't think there are any aliens at all," said Rourke between hands of poker. Rourke was a big redhead with a craggy scar across his forehead. "I think the Sons of Korhal finally found enough tech to avenge the nuking of their homeworld."

"Bite your tongue," said Maggs, a crusty old bird from one of the local dailies. "Even joking about the Korholes is enough to get you shot."

"So you have a theory, man?" countered Rourke.

"They're human, but not our type of human," said the old reporter. "They're from Old Earth. I figure that while we were gone they got so wrapped up in genetic purity and such that they are nothing but clones now, and that they've come after us to clear out the rest of the race."

Rourke nodded. "I heard that one. And Thaddeus

from the *Post* thinks they're robots, and they have some programming that prevents them from defending themselves. That's why they booked out when the *Norad* took them on."

"You're all wrong," said Murray, a stringer from one of the religious networks. "They're angels, and Judgment Day has arrived."

Both Rourke and Maggs made derisive noises, then Rourke said. "What about you, Liberty? What do you think they are?"

"All I know is what I saw," Mike said. "And what I saw was that whatever they are, they liquefied the surface of the planet next door, and they could be here faster than the Confederacy could react. And we're here at ground zero, playing cards."

A pall hung over the table for a moment, and even Murray the holy stringer was quiet. Finally Rourke let out a long breath and said, "You Tarsonis boys sure know how to squelch a good party. You in or out for the next deal?"

Mike suddenly sat up, staring intently out into the road. Despite themselves, Murray and Rourke swiveled in their chairs but could see only the usual handful of marines in the street, some in combat armor, some in regulation uniform.

"Quick, Rourke. Give me your press credentials," Mike said.

The big redhead instinctively grabbed the tags around his neck as though they were a life preserver. "No way, man."

"Okay, then let me trade my credentials for yours." Mike held out his own marine-issued ID.

"How come?" Rourke asked, already pulling the chain off over his head.

"You're local press," Mike said. "They'll let you out of the cordon into the hinterland."

"Yeah, but anything I put down goes through the censors anyway," the big man protested, handing over the tags. "Nothing gets out of here."

"Yeah, but I'm going to go crazy hanging out here. Pack of cigs, too."

"I thought you were quitting, man," Rourke said.

"Come on, man."

As soon as Mike had Rourke's cigarettes jammed in his shirt pocket he was up and out of the café, his own press tags still bouncing on the table.

"They breed them crazy on Tarsonis, man," Rourke observed.

"You going to talk or deal?" Maggs asked.

"Lieutenant Swallow!" Mike shouted. He strung Rourke's tags around his neck as he ran, his boots kicking up plumes of dust in the street.

The lieutenant turned and smiled at him. "Mr. Liberty. It is good to see you again." Her smile was warm, though Mike could not tell if the warmth was heartfelt or the result of her reprogramming.

She wasn't in her combat armor anymore, but rather in regulation khakis. That meant she wasn't on MP duty and it was unlikely she would be actively monitored. Still, she had a small slugthrower on one hip and a nasty-looking combat knife on the other.

Mike reached up and pulled the cigarette pack from his pocket. Swallow smiled guiltily and pulled one out.

"I thought you were quitting," she said.

Mike shrugged. "I thought you were, too."

Mike suddenly realized that he didn't have any matches, but Swallow produced a small lighter. A tiny laser ignited the tip's end.

The lieutenant took a long drag and said, "I am sorry about that thing back on the ship. Duty."

Mike shrugged again. "My job is sometimes asking tough questions. Duty. The bruises have healed. You busy?"

"Not at the moment. Is there a problem, sir?"

"I need a lift and a driver for out into the hinterland." Mike made it sound like a simple request. Like bumming a cigarette.

Swallow's face clouded for a moment. "They're letting you out of the cordon? Nothing personal, sir, but I thought the colonel was going to personally kick your backside to Tarsonis after that incident on the bridge."

"Time wounds all heels," said Mike, pulling up Rourke's tags. "They're lengthening my chain a bit. Just a bit of background stuff—talking to the potential refugees."

"Evacuees, sir," corrected Swallow.

"My point exactly. Have to get a line on the brave

people of Mar Sara in the face of the threat from space. You interested in shuttling me around?"

"Well, I'm off duty, sir . . ." Swallow hesitated, and Mike touched the cigarette pack again. "I can't see the harm. You sure the colonel is down with this?"

Mike beamed a winning, wise smile. "If he isn't, then we get turned back at the first checkpoint, and I'll introduce you to my card-playing buddies at the café."

Lieutenant Swallow wangled transport, an open-topped, wide-bodied jeep. Rourke's tags got them through the checkpoint, a bored MP swiping the card through the reader and getting a green light for the "local reporter." The authorities didn't seem to be horribly worried about people getting out into the hinterlands, particularly those with a military escort. They seemed to be more concerned about people getting back in.

Mar Sara had always been only borderline habitable, in comparison to the formerly rich jungles of its sister in farther orbit. Its sky was a dusty orange, and most of its soil varied between hard-baked mud and stringy scrub. Irrigation had made parts of this desert bloom, but as they passed outside the city Mike could see fields already blighted by lack of water. Watering cranes stood like lonely scarecrows over the brown-tinged crops.

Such crops needed constant attention, Mike noted in his recorder, and the displacement of the population was as deadly for them as an assault from space. The abandonment of the agricultural areas was a sure sign that the Confederates expected the Protoss to return.

They came across their first concentration point for refugees (sorry, evacuees) about midafternoon. It was a fabric city erected in one of the fields, a single Goliath walker overseeing the entire complex. Another bored MP didn't even bother to listen to Mike's full story before swiping Rourke's card through the reader and, being informed that Mike was a local, let him in.

Swallow parked the jeep at the feet of the Goliath.

"Let me talk to the ref . . . evacuees alone," Mike said.

"Sir, I am still responsible for your safety," Swallow responded.

"So watch from a safe distance. People aren't going to open up too well when one of the Confederacy's own is standing there in full kit."

Swallow's face clouded, and Mike added, "Of course, anything I get will go through your people before it gets transmitted." That seemed to reassure her enough to keep her near the jeep while Mike went out to soak up the local color.

The evacuee station was only a few days old, but its facilities were already stressed. It appeared to have been built and supplied for maybe a hundred families, and it currently housed five hundred. Already the overflow of the population was being bundled into square-bodied buses for transportation to other, farther sites. Trash was piling up around the fringes, and there were lines at the water buffaloes for purified water.

The evacuees themselves were just getting over the shock of being dispossessed. Most had been rousted from their homes and managed to take only what they could lay their hands on. As a result, unneeded and sentimental items were being abandoned or traded away for food and warm bedding. Now, at rest for the first time in days, the evacuees had time to take stock of their situation, and assign blame.

Unsurprisingly, the Confederacy came in for most of the blame. After all, they were the only ones on hand, with their Goliath walkers and combat-suited marines a very visible presence. The Protoss, on the other hand, were a rumor, the only proof of them reports from the Confederacy itself. Mar Sara had been on the other side of the sun, so its people missed much of the light show that had destroyed their sister planet.

Mike cataloged the evacuees' plight and listened to the complaints. There were stories of separations and of valuables left behind, reports of farms and homes commandeered by the Confederate forces, and all manner of complaints, major and minor, against the military forces that had replaced all the civilian authorities. The local magistrate had become a refugee himself, leading one pack of refugees to another concentration point. No one was willing to stand up to the Confederates, but the refugees were angry enough to complain to a reporter about it.

Yet under the complaints and bluff talk, there was noticeable and definite fear. There was fear of the Confederate forces, natch, but also fear that arose from the realization that suddenly mankind was no longer alone. The Mar Sarans had seen the reports of the destruction of Chau Sara, and they were afraid that it would happen here. There was a lot of anxious·ness in the camp, and a great desire to be someplace—anyplace—else.

And there was something else there as well, Mike discovered as he moved among the uprooted populace. The sudden knowledge of the Protoss was followed by a wave of mysterious sightings. Lights were reported in the sky, and strange-looking creatures on the ground. Cattle were found slain and mutilated. Add to that the blanket admission that the Confederacy was definitely herding the populace out of certain areas, as if they knew something they weren't telling people.

The stories of aliens and undiscovered xenomorphs on the ground came up again and again. No one had actually seen them, of course. It was always a friend of a friend of a relative in another camp who saw them, or at least heard of them. The stories were more along the lines of bug-eyed monsters than creatures in shining ships, but then, if someone had seen the Protoss ships, the military would be all over the report in minutes.

After about two hours (and the last of Rourke's cigarettes), Mike padded back to the jeep. Lieutenant Swallow was as he had left her, alert, standing next to the driver's side.

"We have enough," he said. "Thanks for the chance to get out here. We can go."

Swallow didn't move. Instead she was staring at something.

"Lieutenant Swallow?"

"Sir," she said, "I've been watching something curious. May I share it with you?"

"And this curious thing would be?"

"You see that woman over there, the red-haired one in the dark outfit?"

Mike looked. There was a woman, young, dressed in what looked like night-camo pants, dark shirt, and a multipocketed vest. She had brilliant red hair that was bound in a ponytail at the nape of her neck. She looked quasi-military, though not from any unit that Mike had ever seen. Maybe some planetary militia or law-enforcement organization. Marshals, that's what the locals called the lawmen, but she didn't look much like one. Mike suddenly realized that he hadn't seen anything of the local law since the marines landed, and had just assumed they had been sucked into the general evacuation.

"Yeah?" he said.

"She's suspicious, sir."

"What's she doing?"

"The same thing you've been doing, sir. Talking to people."

"Well, *that's* definitely suspicious. Shall we go talk to *her?*"

The red-haired woman rose from her most recent conversation with an elderly man and crossed the compound. Swallow strode off toward her, Mike in tow.

As they closed, Mike noticed something else suspicious about the woman: she looked significantly less dusty than the rest of the refugees. And less worried.

"Excuse me, ma'am," Swallow said.

The red-haired woman hesitated in mid-stride and looked around. "Can I help you?" she asked. Her jade-green eyes narrowed just a hair, and Mike noticed that her lips were just a tad too wide for her face.

"We have a few questions," the lieutenant said, perhaps more bluntly than Mike would have liked.

The wide lips pursed, and the woman asked, "And *who* would be asking these questions?" A cold wind seemed to pass between the women as she spoke.

Mike interposed himself between the two. "I'm a reporter for the Universe News Network. My name is Michael . . ."

"Liberty," finished the red-haired woman. "I've seen your reports. They get things right more often than not."

Mike nodded. "They're always right when I finish them. If something went wrong, I blame my editors."

The woman gave Mike a piercing stare, and he was positive she could turn those green eyes into sharp blades that could carve deep into his soul. "I'm Sarah Kerrigan," she said simply, to Mike, not to the lieutenant.

Okay, thought Mike. *Not local law at all.*

"And where are you from, Miss Kerrigan?" asked Lieutenant Swallow. She was still smiling, but Mike could now feel a bit of tension in that smile. Something about this Miss Kerrigan rubbed the lieutenant the wrong way.

"University of Chau Sara," said Kerrigan, looking intently at the officer now. "Part of a sociological team stationed here when the attack came."

"That's a convenient origin," Swallow said, "considering that no one can check on it right now."

"I'm sorry about your planet," put in Mike suddenly. He intended simply to blunt Swallow's tacit accusation, but for the first time he realized that he *was* sorry for the destruction he had seen from orbit. And embarrassed, because he hadn't really thought of it earlier.

The red-haired woman swung her attention back to the reporter. "I know," she said simply. "I feel your sorrow."

"And what are you doing here, Miss Kerrigan?" Swallow was being as blunt as Anderson's favorite letter opener.

Kerrigan replied, "Same as everyone else here, Corporal . . ."

"Lieutenant, ma'am," interrupted Swallow, sharper now.

Kerrigan managed an amused smile. "Lieutenant, then. Trying to find out what's going on. Trying to find out if there's really a plan for evacuation or if the Confeds are running a huge human shell game, here."

"What do you mean by that?" snapped Swallow, but Mike was already rephrasing the question.

"Do you feel there is a problem with the current evacuations?" he put in.

Kerrigan gave a snorting laugh. "Isn't it obvious? You've got bands of people shunted out of the cities and into the hinterlands."

"The cities are not defensible," Swallow noted.

"And the wilderness is?" Kerrigan shot back. "It seems the Confederacy has mistaken activity for progress. They're content to move the refugees around like checkers on the board, without any real plan to evacuate."

"Such plans are in the works, I understand," Mike said calmly.

"I've read the official reports, too," Kerrigan said. "And we both know how much truth there is to them. No, the Confederacy of Man is just chasing its tail right now, moving people around in the hopes that they'll be ready."

"Ready for what?" Mike asked.

"Ready for when the next attack comes," Kerrigan said dryly. "Ready when the next thing goes wrong."

"Ma'am," Swallow said. "I must tell you that the Confederacy is doing as much as is humanly possible to aid the people of Mar Sara."

Kerrigan interrupted hotly. "They are doing as much as is humanly possible to protect themselves, Soldier. The Confederacy has never given a damn beyond the limits of their own bureaucracy. It particularly has never given a damn about its people, and most of all it's never given a damn about anyone not on Tarsonis."

"Ma'am, I must inform you . . ." Swallow began, her smile as brittle as glass.

"I must inform *you* that the Confederacy's history damns it as surely as its current actions do. It's willing to write off the Sara system, just like it wrote off the colonies in the Guild Wars and Korhal itself."

"Ma'am," Swallow said. "I must *warn* you now that we are in a military zone, and dangerous talk will be dealt with swiftly." Mike noticed that Lieutenant Swallow's hand had drifted to the grip of her slug-thrower.

"No, Lieutenant," Kerrigan responded, her eyes blazing, "I must warn *you*. The Confederacy is leading you to the slaughter, and you won't realize it until the knives come out."

Color flushed along Swallow's face. "Don't make me do something you'll regret, ma'am."

"I'm not *making* you do anything," Kerrigan hissed. "It's the bastards in the Confederacy that *make* people do things. They reach inside you and twist you apart until you're their plaything! So the question is: Are you going to follow the programming they gave you, or not?"

Mike stepped back, suddenly aware that the two women were about to come to blows. He looked around, but it seemed that the rest of the camp was paying them no attention.

For a long moment the two women stood, their eyes locked. Finally, Lieutenant Swallow blinked, stepped back, and pulled her hand from the gun butt.

"I *must* assure you, ma'am," said Lieutenant Swallow, her face now ashen, "that you are in error. The Confederacy is only thinking of its people."

"If you *must* assure me, then you *must*," Kerrigan said, snapping off the words. "Will there be anything else, or am I free to engage in an illusion of freedom?"

"No, ma'am. You can go. Sorry to have disturbed you."

"It's nothing." Kerrigan's sharp green eyes softened for a moment. She turned to Mike. "In answer to your next question, you'll find some answers at Anthem Base. It's about three klicks west of here. But don't go alone." She shot a look at the lieutenant.

And then she was gone, striding across the compound and quickly losing herself among the tents.

"The woman was under stress," Swallow said through clenched teeth. She reached up with one hand and pulled a stimpack from her belt.

"Of course," Mike agreed.

"Its not surprising for people to blame their rescuers for their problems," she continued, pressing the pack against the knobby flesh at the back of her neck. The stimpack hissed softly.

"Right."

"And this was not the place or time for an incident." Slowly the color returned to her face, and she started breathing regularly.

"Not the place at all."

"And it would be best not reported," she said firmly.

Mike thought of Swallow's former hobby. "Of course," he said.

"We should go now," said Lieutenant Emily Jameson Swallow, turning back to the jeep.

"Uh-huh," Mike said, scratching his chin and looking at the place where Kerrigan had disappeared. He thought of chasing after her but realized that he would probably not even find her again, unless she wanted to be found. He wanted to ask her about a lot of things.

Particularly about how she knew what his next question was.

He *was* going to ask about the xenomorph sightings. *That* was the next question he was going to ask. This Kerrigan could have known that from talking to the same people that he had been interviewing.

Or it could have been something else about Kerrigan that let her know what he was thinking.

Regardless, as he loped to catch up to Lieutenant Swallow, he resolved never to get into a card game with Sarah Kerrigan.

CHAPTER 5

ANTHEM BASE

Nature abhors a vacuum, and human nature hates a lack of information. Where we can't find it, we go looking for it. In some cases we just invent it.

That was the case on the Sara system. Willfully ignorant, we charged into the hinterland looking for answers—answers that we soon realized we didn't want to find.

We were stupid to assume that we would be all right. We were stupid to go off half-cocked. We were stupid to go in undergunned. We were stupid to think that we understood what we were getting into.

And we were most stupid of all to assume that the Protoss were the first alien race that humanity had met.

—THE LIBERTY MANIFESTO

IT TOOK SOME CAJOLING TO GET LIEUTENANT Swallow to detour to Anthem Base. He told her what he had learned in the camp from the other evacuees, couched in neutral terms so as not to rattle her further.

Even so, the Kerrigan woman had shaken the soldier badly, and now Swallow drove with a wordless intensity across the back roads beyond the camp. The stimpack had given her control over her anger but did not eliminate it entirely.

A rooster's plume of dust churned in their wake, and Michael Liberty was sure that the inhabitants of Anthem would see them coming.

Yet when they got there, the town was empty.

"Looks like they've evacuated," Mike said, dismounting.

Lieutenant Swallow just grunted and moved to the back of the jeep. Opening a hatch, she pulled out a gauss rifle.

"Want one, sir?" she asked.

Mike shook his head.

"Pistol, at least?"

He shook his head again and headed for the nearest building.

It was a mining town, nothing more than about a dozen buildings made of local wood and preformed construction pods. It had become a ghost town. No livestock, no dogs, not even birds.

So why, wondered Mike, did he get the feeling he was being watched?

The first building was a claims office. Wooden floor, quarters in the back. The place looked as if its occupants had just left it. There were still blue crystals resting on the scales on a counter-top.

Mike walked in. Swallow lingered at the door, her

oversized weapon at the ready. There was an acrid smell in the air.

"They've evacuated," she said. "We should do the same."

Mike picked up a coffeepot. It had been boiled to a solid sludge, and the pot itself was warm to the touch.

"This is still on," he said, pulling the plug from the hot plate.

"They left in a hurry, sir," Swallow said, a nervous tone now creeping into her voice. "You said the evacuees were complaining of being shuttled off."

Mike walked behind the counter and pulled open a drawer. "There's still money in the till. Can't imagine any assayer leaving his cash behind. Or the marines not giving him a chance to recover it. Odd." He disappeared into the back room.

Swallow shouted after him, and he reappeared.

"Somebody's quarters. Looks like there was a struggle there," he said.

"Unwilling evacuee," Swallow said, looking hard at Mike. "They probably dragged him off before he had a chance to close up his shop."

Mike nodded. "Let's check the other buildings. You take one side. I'll take the other."

Lieutenant Swallow took a deep breath. "As you wish, sir. But stay in the doorways where I can see you."

Mike crossed the street to the opposite line of buildings. A fresh breeze kicked up, and dust devils swirled down the main street of Anthem. The place was completely deserted by both man and beast.

Then why, wondered Mike, did the hairs on the back of his neck still bristle?

Across from the claims office were a pair of residences. Like the assayer's office, they seemed only recently deserted. A video screen was active in one, flickering soundlessly with a bad transmission of a news report. Stock footage of a battlecruiser, identified as the *Norad II*, cruising effortlessly through space.

There was a spilled can of beer next to the easy chair in front of the video. Despite himself, Mike found himself checking to see if any cigarettes had been left behind. No such luck.

The third building was a general mercantile, and it looked as if it had been ransacked. Bins had been overturned and products pulled from the racks and strewn across the floor. Behind the register a large glass gun case had been smashed open. The guns were missing.

Perhaps this was what Sarah Kerrigan wanted him to find, thought Michael. The signs of an armed struggle. Against the Confederacy's evacuation? Or against the Protoss?

Mike looked over his shoulder to see Swallow crossing to a two-story tavern on her side of the road. He stepped into the mercantile, and his foot struck something crunchy.

Mike knelt down. The floor was covered with some type of mold or fungus. It was a dark grayish substance, its edges crusty but slightly elastic to the touch. It contained a spiderweb pattern of darker bands, almost like arteries.

Something had spilled here, and some type of native mold had taken quick advantage of it. Very quick, he realized—it could not have happened more than two days ago.

There was something else about the mercantile. There was a sound from the back of the store, the sound of something sliding over the wooden floorboards. It shifted once, then was silent.

A wild animal? Mike wondered. A snake? Or perhaps a refugee who had escaped the initial evacuation, or returned later. Mike took another step into the room, the fungus crunching under his boots.

He was suddenly very aware that he didn't have a weapon on him.

Swallow gave a shout from across the street. Mike looked at the door to the back room once, then back to Swallow. He backed out of the general store and crossed over to the bar. Swallow was plastered against the wall outside the door.

"I think there's something over in the store—" Mike said.

"I found the inhabitants," Swallow hissed. The veins were pounding along the scars in her neck and thundered at her temples, and her eyes were wide. She was terrified, and the fear was eating into her resocialization programming. It was clear that she had hit the stimpack again, as the discharged unit now lay on the porch floorboards.

Despite himself, Mike looked through the open doorway in the bar.

It had been transformed into an abattoir. Once-human forms hung by their feet from thick ropes attached to the ceiling. Many had been stripped of clothing and flesh. Others had had limbs removed, and three had been decapitated. The three skulls were set along the bar, and had been neatly carved open to reveal the brains beneath. Something had been gnawing on one of the brains.

As he watched, something like a gigantic centipede writhed around on one of the bodies. It was like a huge, rust-colored maggot. And it was feeding on the flesh.

Mike suddenly found it very hard to breathe, and wished he had a stimpack. He took a step into the room.

His feet crunched on the crusty fungus that covered the room. And he realized that he was not alone.

He felt its presence before he saw it. The sudden feeling of being watched returned.

He started to step back, out of the doorway. He started to turn. He started to say something to Swallow.

Something blurred from behind the bar, bolting forward in a single impossible leap, barreling for the doorway.

It didn't hit Mike. Instead, something larger slammed him to one side.

Mike hit the porch floorboards with a thump and

twisted to see Lieutenant Swallow, who had struck him, firing at a large dog in the street. No, it wasn't a dog. It had four legs, but the similarity ended there. Patches of orange-shaded flesh were skinless, muscles showing through. Its head was adorned with a pair of huge, underslung tusks.

And it was screaming under the barrage of metal spikes from the gauss rifle. The hypersonic rounds riddled it in a dozen places, and it flailed in the dirt as Swallow kept her finger clenched on the trigger.

"Swallow!" shouted Mike, "It's dead! Lieutenant Swallow, quit firing!"

Swallow let go of the trigger housing as though it were a live snake. Sweat rolled down her face, and the sides of her mouth were flecked with foam. She was breathing hard, and despite herself, her free hand went for her knife.

Mike realized that her resocialization had been stressed to its utmost, and she was about to lose it.

"Sweet Mother of Christ," she said. "What *is* that!"

Mike didn't care. Instead he shouted, "Back to the jeep! We'll send armored troops! Come on!"

He took two steps, then realized that Swallow was still in the doorway, staring at the skinned dog-thing in the street.

"Lieutenant! That's an order, dammit!" bellowed Mike.

That did it. The beauty of resocialization was that it made its subject vulnerable to orders, particularly under the effect of stims. Swallow suddenly was back in control, running toward the jeep, passing Mike. There was movement from the mercantile as they ran. More of the dog-things were coming through the doorway. They could leap prodigiously, Mike realized, and could strike them in the back as they fled.

The dog-things didn't. Instead the creatures waited for them almost to reach the jeep when *something else* rose up behind the vehicle.

To Mike it was a snake, a cobra rearing to strike. A snake with an armored head that flared out backward in a broad frill of bony chitin like a prehistoric lizard's. It was a snake with two arms jutting from its body, arms that ended in wicked-looking scythes.

Scythes that now drove into the hood of the jeep, pinning it to the street. The snake-creature let out a hissing cry of victory.

Swallow cursed. "They've got us surrounded!"

Mike grabbed her by the sleeve. "The claims office. It has one entrance! Make for it!"

He headed in that direction, the soldier hot on his heels. Behind him he heard more gunfire and the screams of the dog-things. Swallow was backpedaling and firing at the same time, covering their butts as they fled.

He paused in the doorway of the office and quickly scanned the room. Nothing had changed since he had been there moments before. He ran for the counter and came up with a primitive shotgun. He broke it open and found a pair of rounds chambered.

Yeah, the office had been left as if its owner had been called away suddenly. Or dragged away.

Swallow was in the doorway, firing bursts. There were more inhuman screams, then silence.

He looked out the doorway to see a half-dozen bodies in the street, all of them dog-things. Now they looked even less like normal animals than before, the uninjured portions of their bodies riven with pustules and knotted muscles. One of them still twitched a leg in a pool of gelatin that could have been its blood.

Of the snake-thing with the scythes there was no sign. The jeep was a crumpled husk at the end of the street, its leaking fuel darkening the sand beneath it.

"Those were the things that killed Chau Sara?" Swallow hissed the question, her voice a strangled whisper. Her eyes were practically orbs of pure white.

Mike shook his head. The things they had seen in space had a frightful beauty about them. They were gold and silver and seemed to be made of lightning and elemental power itself. These things were nothing but muscle and blood and madness. It hurt him even to look at them.

"Oh Christ, where is the big one?" Swallow asked.

Mike choked back the dust and the fear. "We have to get out of here before they regroup."

Swallow turned toward him, wide-eyed and panicked. "Out of here? We just got here!"

"They're going to regroup and try again."

"They're animals," she snapped, and the tip of her

gauss rifle rose slightly toward Mike. "Shoot a few, the rest will run."

"I don't think so. Animals don't hang up their kills. They don't take trophies."

Swallow gave a short, strangled cry and stepped back into the office. "No, don't say that."

"Swallow. Emily, I . . ."

"Don't say that," she said, stepping back again. "Don't say that they're intelligent. Because if they are, they know we're trapped, and they know they can take us whenever they want to. Dammit, we're fu—"

She took another step backward, and the floorboards gave way beneath her. She let out a strangled scream, and the gun fell from her hands as a pit opened beneath her feet.

From deep within the pit, there was the sound of angry chittering.

Swallow twisted as she fell, grabbing the floorboards to break her fall. The chittering grew louder.

Mike stepped forward, almost dropping his own weapon. "Emily, grab my hand!"

"Get out of here, Liberty!" Swallow snarled, her eyes almost all white from fear. With her free hand she grabbed her combat knife. "Oh God, they're right underneath us!"

"Emily, grab my hand!"

"Someone has to get back," she said, pulling her knife free and hacking at something unseen within the pit. "They're going to attack from above as well. Get going! Hump it back to the camp. Warn people!"

"I can't—"

"Move! That's an order, dammit!" Swallow was snarling as the last of her resocialization shattered beneath the creatures' assault. She let out a feral scream and started flailing with her knife.

Mike turned back to the door, and there was a shadow there. Without thinking, he pulled both triggers on the shotgun, and was splattered by ichor of the exploding dog-thing.

Then he ran. Not looking back, he ran, throwing the spent shotgun aside as he fled. Toward the jeep. Lieutenant Swallow had pulled the rifle out of a hatch in the back. She had offered him one. It had to be there still. Other weapons as well.

He nearly made it when the ground erupted beneath the jeep.

The armor-headed snake-thing, with the scythe arms. It had been waiting for him.

Mike sprawled out of the way of the eruption and started crawling backward, away from the serpent-thing. He was trapped in the creature's eyes, luminous yellow eyes set deep beneath its armored carapace.

There was intelligence in those eyes, and hunger. But nothing that resembled a soul.

The creature rose on its tail, towering over the shattered jeep, ready to leap forward. Mike threw his arm over his face and screamed.

His cries were drowned out by the sound of a gauss rifle on full auto.

Mike looked up to see the huge serpent-beast twist

and shudder under a relentless volley of rifle spikes. As it writhed, it shot spines from its armored body that peppered the surrounding ground like deadly rain.

Then a round found the remaining fuel in the jeep, and the entire vehicle went up, taking the serpent-thing with it. It bellowed something that might have been a curse and might have been a cry to some unknown god.

The explosion pressed Mike backward against the ground, and the warmth of the fire beat against his exposed face and arms. He looked down the street. No sign of the dog-creatures. Only corpses.

There was a sound behind him, and he spun in place, still on the ground. He expected more dog-things, but he knew he was wrong even as he turned. It was the sound of booted feet, not callused paws.

A large, thankfully human figure blocked the sunlight. Broad-shouldered, and packing a heavy slug-thrower from a belt holster worn low on his hip. Dizzily, Mike thought at first the shadow belonged to another of Swallow's unit, that the lieutenant had somehow managed to call in reinforcements when they had split up.

As his vision cleared, Mike realized the figure wasn't in marine uniform. His pants were buckskin leather, well-worn and rough. He was wearing a denim shirt, neat but faded, rolled up at the sleeves. A lightweight combat vest, made of some open, leathery weave, pegged him as some kind of military. So did the gauss rifle he was packing. His boots were well-made but as worn as the rest of his outfit.

"You all right, son?" The silhouette held out a hand.

Mike grabbed the hand and gently rose to his feet. He felt like one great bruise, and the figure's voice sounded distant and tinny in his ears.

"Fine. Alive," he gasped. "You're not a marine."

He could see his rescuer's face now. A head of sandy blond hair and a neatly trimmed mustache and beard.

The figure spat into the dust. "Not a marine? I guess I'll take that as a compliment. I'm the local law in these parts. Marshal Jim Raynor."

"Michael Liberty. UNN, Tarsonis."

"Newsman?" Raynor asked. Mike nodded. "Kind of far from home, aren't you?"

"Yeah. We were checking out a report. . . . Oh God."

"What?"

"Swallow! The lieutenant! I left her in the claims office!" Mike staggered toward the assayer's office. The lawman followed close behind, his weapon ready. In the aftermath of the explosion, there was no further sign of the dog-things.

Mike found Lieutenant Swallow facedown, still half in the pit, one hand still gripping her combat knife, the other clutched tightly to a loose floorboard.

The marshal looked at the room and said, "Son." It had a warning tone.

"Give me a hand here," Mike said, grabbing Swallow's knife arm, "We can haul her up and . . . Oh God."

Lieutenant Emily Jameson Swallow no longer existed below the waist. Her flesh ended in stringy tatters of meat, and a few vertebrae dangled from a torn spinal cord like beads on a broken string.

"Oh God." Mike let go of the body. It slid back into the pit with a sick, slithering sound. There was a squishy thump, and the sound of something else moving below.

Mike fell to his knees, leaned forward, and puked his guts out. Then a second time and a third, until all he had was dry heaves. His head spun, and he felt as if something had sucked all the blood out of his brain.

"Not to interrupt," said Raynor, "but I think we need to go. I think all I did was take out one of their officers. Fragging the captain, if you take my meaning. They're regrouping. We'd better go. I got a bike outside." He paused for a moment, then said, "Sorry about your friend."

Mike nodded, and felt his stomach make one last attempt to empty itself.

"Yeah," Mike gasped at last. "Me, too."

CHAPTER 6

CREEPS

War is easy to understand on paper. It seems so distant and academic in black and white. Even the vid reports have a cool, detached manner that keeps the viewer from understanding how horrible it really is.

This is nothing more than a sanity filter, allowing those that take in the information to separate the reports and numbers from the awful reality. It's why those who lead armies can do all sorts of terrible things to their troops that no sane man would think of if he had to look them in the eye. Which is one reason they don't.

But when you're confronted with death, when you're confronted with having to deal out death or die yourself, then everything changes.

The filters drop away, and you have to deal with the insanity directly.

THE LIBERTY MANIFESTO

"THEY CALL 'EM THE ZERG," SAID MARSHAL Raynor, climbing onto his hover-cycle. "The little ones are called zerglings. The snaky one we blew up is called a hydralisk. They're supposed to be slightly smarter than the small ones."

Mike's mouth still felt as if he had been gargling garbage water, but he said, "Who calls them those things? Who named them the Zergs?"

Raynor replied, "The marines. That's where I heard it from."

"Figures. Those marines mention anything about something called the Protoss?"

"Yep," Raynor said, strapping the reporter in. "They have shining ships and blew up Chau Sara. May be coming here, too, I understand. That's why everyone is beating feet for the exits."

"Think they're one and the same?"

"Don't know. You?"

Mike shrugged. "I saw their ships over Chau Sara. I'd be surprised to discover that these . . . things . . . were at the helm. Maybe their allies? Maybe slaves?"

"Possible. It's better than the alternative."

"And that is?"

"That they're enemies," said the lawman, firing up the hover-cycle's main plant. "That would be much worse for anybody caught between them."

They circled the dead town of Anthem Base one last time. Liberty recorded the devastation on his comm unit as Raynor fired fragmentation grenades into the wooden structures. They left a pillar of smoke behind them.

Raynor explained that he was riding scout for a

group of refugees. Local government types. They were another few klicks farther along, heading for a place called Backwater Station.

"There's a refugee camp about three klicks back that way." Mike motioned toward the rear. "Aren't you heading that way?"

"Nope. There was a report of trouble up at Backwater, and we went to investigate it."

"No mention of a refugee camp at all in your report?" Mike asked.

"Nope. Of course, it *does* seem like the Confederacy wants to have most of the planetary population running around like chickens with their fool heads cut off."

"Somebody else said that to me just before we came here."

"Whoever told you that," Raynor said approvingly, "has his head screwed on right."

They flew smoothly over the rough terrain, Raynor changing course only to veer around the larger obstacles. The Vulture hover-cycle was a long-nosed bike with limited gravity hover technology that kept it a foot above the ground. The onboard computer and sensors in the nose kept it at a steady pace, ignoring the smaller boulders and scrub trees.

Strapped in on the back, Mike thought, *I gotta get one of these . . . and a decent set of battle armor.* He thought again of Lieutenant Swallow and wondered how she would have fared had she been wearing her insulating cocoon of neosteel.

They caught up with Raynor's pack of refugees within the hour. The marshal was right: this particular gathering had been the local government types, conveniently sent into the wilderness on marine orders. Mike could imagine Colonel Duke's delight in issuing *that* particular communication. The march had been brought to a halt, and Raynor accosted one of the rear guard.

"Something ahead we hadn't counted on," said the soldier, one of the colonial troops in CMC-300 armor. "Looks like an old command post."

"One of ours?" Raynor asked.

"Kinda. It wasn't on any maps of the area. We sent the rest of the scout unit up to check it out."

Raynor twisted around in his seat. "You want off?" he asked Mike.

"Off the planet, yeah," Mike said. "But as long as I have to be here I want to take a look. It's the job. Duty." He thought of Anthem Base and didn't trust old buildings all of a sudden.

Raynor grunted an agreement and gunned the bike forward. They crested a low hill and found the command post on the other side.

Michael knew what to expect from command posts. They were ubiquitous, even on Tarsonis. Half-domes filled with sensor equipment and computers, they were little more than small automatic factories that ground out construction vehicles to work the local mines, and would not have much in the way of either a staff or a defense. Some brilliant developer along the way put jumpjets on the bottom of the structures to move them where needed, but if you ever had to move them, you had to shut everything else down.

This one was, well, different. It seemed a bit mashed along one side. Not damaged from without, but rather shrunken from within, like an apple that had been left in the sun too long. The sides were overgrown with briers and tangles. In a half-circle around it, the colonial forces, green local troops in worn combat armor, were cautiously approaching.

"Never saw anything like that before," Raynor said. "All overgrown and such. For it to look that bad, it would have to have been here before the colony was settled."

Mike looked at the ground around the base of the command post. He pointed. "Look there!"

"What?"

"The ground. It's got that creeping gray stuff around it. We found it in Anthem before the Zergs attacked."

"Think it's connected?"

"Oh, yeah." Mike nodded in agreement.

"Good enough for me," said the marshal, flipping over the comm mike on his bike. "That building's been infested with Zerg, boys. Let 'em have it!"

Mike kept his own recorder open and said, "Tell them to look out for the zerglings. They like to burrow."

He didn't need to give the warning. The ground in

front of the command center opened up and spilled forth a double-handful of the skinned-dog creatures. The colonial forces were prepared, and mowed them down as soon as they appeared. The zerglings didn't stand a chance, and were reduced to pulpy husks in the first volleys. Having dealt with the initial threat, the local militia then fired incendiary rounds into the command post itself. The building started to burn.

Raynor stayed on the bike, firing fragmentation grenades from a stubby launcher until the roof cracked open like a shattered eggshell. Mike got a good look within: the entire structure was nothing more than a tangle of pestilent vines, a riot of orange, green, and violet. Sacs of messy proto-*somethings* were hanging along one wall. They screamed as the fire reached them.

"You're getting all that?" Raynor asked as the roof caved in, burying the smoking relics of the infested building beneath it.

"Yeah." Mike closed his recording unit. "Now I need someplace to patch in for a report."

Raynor smiled. "I told you, this band of refugees are government types. If anyone has a decent comm system, it'll be them."

Marshal Raynor was right. The refugees did have a more-than-adequate comm link, and in normal times it would be a smooth link. But as he logged on, it was obvious to Mike that parts of the system were going down worldwide. There were obvious holes in the net, and a high level of background noise. Like the farms, the communications network was being forcibly ignored, with immediate ramifications.

He crafted the tale as best he could, wondering what the military censors would pull out before giving it to UNN, and what Handy Anderson would change. The viewing populace, and all the steps in between, needed to know what was going on, regardless.

He packed most of the material from the refugee camp as a sidebar, but said nothing of the altercation between Swallow and Kerrigan. He went into detail about the situation at Anthem Base and provided footage of the firing of the command post. He closed with a note that the command post was not on any colonial maps, confident that the censors would pull that line, if they felt they had to pull anything.

He was also sure they would let run the shots of the brave colonial forces mowing down the zerglings. Triumphant actions like that always played well with the military censors.

As the report percolated through the buffer into the general net, Mike pounded the orange dust out of his coat. Then he hunted down Raynor in the mess tent. The sandy-haired man offered him a cup of coffee. It was military style "B"—boiled to a thickened sludge and allowed to cool. It was like drinking soft asphalt.

"You get off your report?" asked the lawman.

"Uh-huh," Mike replied. "Even remembered to spell your name right." He flashed a brittle grin

"You okay?" Raynor asked. It came out "yokay."

Mike shrugged. "I'll hold up. Writing helps me work through it."

"You've seen death before, right?"

Mike shrugged again. "On Tarsonis? Sure. Random shootings. Suicides. Gang hits and auto accidents. Even some things that would rival those bodies hung up in the tavern." He took a deep breath. "But I'll admit, never anything like this. Not like the lieutenant."

"Yeah, it's tough when you were talking to the victim moments before it happened," said Raynor, taking another slug of asphalt. "And when it's sudden. And just so you know, the answer is no, it wasn't your fault."

"How could you know that?" Mike asked, suddenly irritated. He had been thinking exactly that: that he was responsible for bringing Swallow to Anthem and to her death.

"I know because I'm a marshal. And while I've never seen anything quite like Anthem Base, I've been in situations where some people live, and some die. And the living feel guilty about still being alive. Afterwards."

Mike sat there for a moment. "What do you recommend, then, Doctor Raynor?"

Raynor shrugged. "Pretty much what you're doing. Get on with your life. Do what you have to do. Don't get strung out. You got rattled, but you're shaking it off."

Mike nodded. "You know, speaking of getting on with life, there's one thing I've been meaning to do."

"And that is . . . ?"

"Learn to use that combat armor. I passed on the chance when I was flying around with the fleet, and I've been regretting it ever since. Seems like it might be a survival skill around here."

"That it is." Raynor looked over his mug at the reporter. "Yeah, I think we got a spare two-hundred-level suit. And we're going to be encamped here until we hear from the marines. It might be a good time to learn."

A half hour later Mike was suited up outside the mess tent. It had taken ten minutes to scare up the suit from all the cargo that the evacuees had brought along, and another twenty to suit him properly. He knew that Swallow could slip into her suit in three minutes, tops. *Crawl before you can walk*, Mike told himself.

The suit itself was similar to the powered combat suits used by the *Norad II* crew. It was invulnerable to small-arms fire, had limited life-support (as opposed to the full space-traveling suits of the marines), and packed basic nuclear/biological/chemical shielding. Still, it was an earlier model than standard marine issue, practically an antique. Apparently the local law got hand-me-downs from the Confederate government.

The complete suit raised Mike's height by a full foot, the oversized boots containing their own stabilization computers to keep him upright. The suit also rode a little high in the crotch, as well, until Raynor showed him where the lever was to raise the foot supports. The suit could be sealed, and it would run for seven days on its own recycled waste. That was a thrill that Mike could pass on for the moment.

The shoulders were oversized as well, housing ammunition reloads and sensor arrays. The backpack was an oversized air conditioner, shunting away heat from the body. The more advanced models carried mufflers to cut down the noise and heat signature, but this was an ancient model, battered and repatched numerous times.

Parts of it seemed a bit tight, snug around the arms and legs in wide bands. Other places seemed loose and open.

"The tight spots are part of the salvage system," said Raynor, strapping him in. "You take a big hit to an arm or leg, the suit seals off in a tourniquet. One piece goes but the rest survives."

"Feels like a hollow spot under the arms," said Mike.

"Yeah, well, this is marine surplus. That's where the stimpacks would be. We don't use them in the colonial militias. Too many people get addicted to the drugs in them." He closed the last latch and sealed Mike in. The reporter swayed back and forth, feeling like a turtle on stilts.

Raynor was in his own suit, looking equally battered and worn. The lawman nodded behind his open visor and said, "The armor will stop most common slugthrowers, though a good needle-gun can still punch through. That's why most front-line troops carry C-14 Impalers, gauss rifles that fire eight-millimeter spikes."

"What now?"

"Now you walk," said Raynor. Several other soldiers were now watching as well, and a small crowd was forming at the entrance to the mess tent. The lawman nodded again. "Go ahead."

Mike looked at the telltales along the rim of his visor. He *had* read the manuals earlier, on the ship, and knew that the small lights meant that everything was hunky-dory. He took a step forward.

He expected the step to be like pulling out of mud, since he was lifting the huge weight of a booted foot. Instead the foot, tethered into sensors and backed by a ton of cabled ligature, came up almost to his waist. High-stepping, Mike overbalanced, leaning backward. The servos whined in response, and he twisted, falling on his side with a resounding thump.

Raynor put a hand to his face, trying to look sage but barely covering the grin that blossomed beneath his fingers. Mike saw that several of the other militiamen were trading money back and forth. *Great, they're betting on this*, thought Mike. The telltales along his visor flashed a warning yellow. He looked at them, consulted the manual in his memory, and decided that they all meant "Hey, dummy, you've fallen over."

"A hand here?" Mike said.

"You're better doing it on your own." There was a smile in Raynor's voice.

Wonderful, thought Mike, slowly rolling onto his

belly. He found he could push himself up on one hand, but moving the oversized legs underneath him was a tight fit. At last he pulled himself up to a near-vertical position.

"Good," Raynor said. "Now walk. Go ahead."

Mike tried shuffling this time, and the armor responded by slogging forward, churning up a cloud of orange dust. He shuffled ahead ten feet, then turned, and shuffled another ten. By the second turn he was confident enough to take real steps, and when he didn't fall down, started moving normally. The tell-tales winked green at him again, and he was relieved that he hadn't damaged the suit. He was also glad he hadn't laughed too hard at the new crewmen during the drills on the *Norad II*.

Raynor went over to the colonial militia and came back with the gauss rifle. He handed it to Mike, and his armored hand closed over the larger of two grips. The smaller grip, used by nonarmored shooters, required the firer to use both hands to steady its long barrel. In the armor, Raynor could heft it easily.

"Take a shot at that boulder," he said, trying valiantly to keep a smile from his face.

At first Mike thought the marshal was only amused by his performance, but as he leveled the gun, he thought about what he was doing. The armored turtle on stilts was about to fire a gun.

"Hang on," he said. "How does this thing handle recoil?"

Raynor turned to the other militiamen. "See? I told you he was smarter than he looked!" Some of the colonial soldiers reached for their wallets.

To Mike he said, "You brace, go into a broad-legged stance. The suit knows the maneuver. It compensates along the gun arm."

Mike turned back toward the boulder, braced himself, and let off a burst. A volley of spikes erupted from the muzzle of the rifle and peppered the boulder. Splinters of rock flew everywhere, and Mike saw that he had carved a white scar across the surface of the stone.

"Not bad," said Raynor, smiling fully now. "That's one rock that's going to think twice about attacking good God-fearing people."

Mike felt as though a load had been lifted from his shoulders. Swallow was dead, and there were strange xenomorphs all over a wilderness filled with refugees. But at least he was doing something about it.

As far as he was concerned, he had made an important, armored, first step.

Raynor's evacuees were supposed to hold tight until the marines contacted them. Mike figured he could hang with Raynor's crew for about a day, maybe two, then either catch a lift back to the city with the marines or find his own ride back. Heck, once news of the colonial marines fighting the Zerg got on the local news, their group might even be bumped forward in the queue.

He didn't worry about the report until late the next day, when the real marines arrived.

They howled down out of the orange sky like steel-shod furies. The Confederate dropships deployed at the cardinal points around the refugee camp, preventing easy escape. As soon as they landed, heavily armored marines in full, modern combat gear piled out, accompanied by firebats, specialty troops armed with plasma-based flame throwers. A single Goliath strode out of the belly of one of the dropships and stood guard over the far end of the camp.

The marines quickly surrounded the encampment and advanced into the refugees' midst. Wherever they met colonial troops, they called for their disarmament and surrender. Surprised and unsure, the colonials complied.

Mike, now dressed in his civilian gear and long duster, headed for Raynor's tent. He got there just as the marshal was shouting at his vidscreen.

"Are you out of your mind? If we *hadn't* burned that damned factory this entire colony could have been overrun! Maybe if you hadn't taken your sweet time in getting here . . ."

"Now I asked you nice the first time, boy," came a familiar voice over the screen that froze Mike's soul. He could not see the face, but he knew that Colonel Duke was at the other end of that vid-link. "I didn't come here to talk with you. Now throw down them weapons!"

Raynor muttered, "Guess you wouldn't be a

Confederate if you weren't a *complete* pain in the ass."
Only then did he toggle the link off. To Mike he said,
"Typical Confed thinking. We do their jobs for them,
so naturally they're peeved at the competition."

A pair of marines in full kit appeared in the doorway. "Marshal James Raynor, we have a warrant for
your arrest for treasonous activities—"

"Yeah, yeah," sighed Raynor. "I got the love note
from your colonel." He placed his sidearms on the
table. They vanished into the possession of the
marine.

"There was also a Michael Liberty of the Universe
News Network present at the time of the assault on
the command post," said the marine, turning toward
Mike.

"Well, he's—" Raynor began.

"Gone," said Mike, holding up his press tags.
"Name's Rourke. Local press. Mickey booked out yesterday after filing his report."

The marine swiped the swapped ID card across a
reader, then grunted. Mike hoped that the patchiness
of global communications prevented Rourke's picture
from coming up.

The marine said, "Mr. Rourke, you are as of this
moment in a restricted area. You must leave at once."

Raynor said, "What the—"

Mike interrupted him. "Of course, sir. I'm gone."

The marine continued, "I must remind you that
under martial law, anything you report of this will be
reviewed by military censors. Any treasonous writings

will be reported, and the writer will be punished to the full extent of the law."

"Right you are, man. I mean, sir," said Mike.

Raynor shouted at Mike, "Hey, 'Rourke,' you'd better take my bike." He tossed the reporter the keys. "It doesn't look like I'm going to be needing it for a while."

"Sure thing, Marshal," said Mike.

The lawman looked hard at Mike. "And if you see that Liberty jasper," he said in a stony voice, "tell him I expect him to do something about this mess. You hear?"

"Loud and clear, man," said Mike. "Loud and clear."

Even so, Mike didn't let himself relax until he was a good five klicks from the refugee encampment. When he left, Raynor's men were being herded into the dropships. If Duke followed standard Confederate military procedure, they would be lifted to a prison hulk in high orbit.

Mike consoled himself with the fact that at least in orbit they would have some protection from the Zerg and the Protoss.

Originally Mike's plan was to get back to the city, catch a ship off-planet, and then let Handy Anderson sort out the details of his unauthorized sojourn once Mike got back to Tarsonis. But the idea of leaving Raynor to rot in some marine prison churned at him. The marshal was one of the aw-shucks good-old-boys who seemed to thrive out here on the Fringe Worlds, but he wasn't a bad sort. And he had saved Mike's bacon at Anthem.

Briefly the face of Lieutenant Swallow rose in his memory. She had helped him, and he had failed her. Despite what Raynor had said, he felt responsible. Would he fail Raynor as well?

"Fail is such an ugly word," he muttered, but he knew he couldn't leave the lawman to Duke's tender mercies. By the time he hit the city limits, he knew he had to get a shuttle to the *Norad II* and have it out with the colonel.

Hell, maybe we'll get adjoining cells, he thought.

The city was completely evacuated now, and there wasn't even a cordon at the main entrances. The streets were abnormally empty, and not even other Confederate troops were present. Flying down the empty streets, Mike wondered what had happened to the café crowd at the press pool. Were they still there, or had they been evacuated to some dump in the wilderness as well?

There was a *whump*, and the Vulture hover-cycle rocked beneath him. Looking back, he saw that another Vulture had crept up on him and nudged his left rear bumper. Behind the polarized window, Mike saw the silhouette of the driver point to his ear. The universal symbol for "Turn on your radio, idiot."

Mike toggled on the comm unit, and Sarah Kerrigan's face appeared on the screen. "Follow me," she said.

"You trying to get me killed?"

"That's a stupid question, considering you're already dead."

"What?!" Mike sputtered.

"A report went out an hour ago. Said that some terrorists in stolen firebat armor strafed a bus full of reporters. They identified the victims by their badges. Congrats, you got top billing in the obituary."

"Oh, God." Mike felt the weight shift in his stomach. Rourke had his press badge. The idea that the construction scandal had finally caught up with him, this far out, crossed his mind.

Kerrigan laughed. "This is no building-supplies scandal back on Tarsonis, newshound. Somebody here wanted you dead. You know too much, Mr. Liberty."

Mike's stomach churned. "What do you mean?"

Frustration crackled over the link. "I mean that your report from the field brought the house down on the local forces. The fact that they are fighting the Zerg and the marines aren't is painfully obvious, so Duke had the local troops arrested and shipped off-planet. He wants the place defenseless. Isn't it obvious? If you really want to help the locals, follow me."

Mike shook his head. "And if I refuse?"

"I'll run you off the road and drag you off," crackled the comm link. "Jeez, you drive like someone's grandmother."

With that Kerrigan pulled her Vulture ahead and took a quick left. Liberty followed, suddenly painfully aware that he took the corners much too wide.

They headed for a district full of warehouses, some of them now nothing more than empty husks. Kerrigan's Vulture slipped into the open door of one of them. Mike pulled his inside as well, and Kerrigan ran down the door behind him.

"Bumping me like that was pretty dangerous," Mike said, dismounting from the Vulture. "You must think yourself a pretty good driver."

"I am. I'm *also* very good with knives. And guns, too. You steal that?" she asked, looking at the bike.

"Got it from a friend."

"Your friend is hard on his equipment. This is a safe house. There's one more thing before we go on."

Before Mike could react, Kerrigan snaked out a hand and grabbed his press tags. With a single smooth motion she tossed them in the air, pulled a hand-held laser, and fried the tags at the top of their arc. The melted remains landed with a sodden *splot* on the concrete floor.

"We think the press tags can be traced. That would explain why bad things happened to the guy with your original tags. Eventually they'll figure out that they left a reporter alive, and they'll come after you then. Now come back here. I have to set up some equipment."

She turned, leaving Mike sputtering. She started moving some equipment in the back.

"Look, you know you can't trust Duke's forces right now, so will you listen to my side, at least?" She bent over to check some plugs.

Mike recognized the equipment. "That's a full holo setup."

"State of the art," Kerrigan said with a smile. "My commander has been fortunate enough to get the best."

"The best indeed, if he can afford to keep his own telepaths."

Kerrigan froze for only a fraction of a second, but enough to make Mike smile. "Yeah, well," she said. "I don't do enough to hide *that*, do I?"

"I was willing to buy your being a big fan of mine," Mike said, "but just *happening* to find me while I was coming into the city, well, that was a bit *too* much to believe. I thought that only Confederate Marine ghost-troopers were telepaths."

"Well, I did that job once. Got tired of it and left."

"I don't need to be a telepath to know there's more to the story than that." Mike shrugged in a disarming way, then added, "It's not a job you retire from. I also thought that telepaths had inhibitors on them to protect us normal folk."

"It's the other way around," said Kerrigan, a taste of bitterness in her voice. "The inhibitors also keep your nasty little thoughts out of *my* mind. It's tough when you know everyone around you is untrustworthy at some level." She looked hard at Mike, her green eyes flashing. "The bathroom's in the back corner. No, it doesn't have a window you can sneak out of. I don't want to shoot your knees out to keep you here, but you know I will."

"Why me?" muttered Mike as he headed for the john.

"Because, you idiot," shouted Kerrigan from across the room, "you're important to us. Now powder your nose and get back here."

When Mike returned she had finished the setup for the holographic rig. It had a full projection plate, but could fit into a couple suitcases.

"It's not, you know," she said as he approached.

"Not an advantage to a reporter to read minds?" Mike was catching onto the odd shorthand of talking to a telepath.

"No." Kerrigan shook her head, "Most of what I get is off the surface, and even that is usually pretty slimy. Animal needs and all that crap. And secrets. Damn it, my entire life has been filled with secrets. It gets real old, real fast."

"Sorry," Mike said, suddenly realizing he didn't know if he meant it or not.

"Yeah, you meant it. You just don't know you meant it. And no, I don't have any cigarettes. Here we go."

She stroked a switch and spoke softly into a microphone. The lower plate of the holographic transmitter whirred softly, and a humanoid aura took form in the light. It seemed to be carved out of the light itself, a massive man, broad-shouldered, in quasi-military uniform. His face resolved into bushy eyebrows, a craggy nose, a huge mustache, and a prominent chin. His hair was black with gray stripes, but still was more black than gray.

Mike recognized him at once from dozens of wanted posters across the Confederacy.

"Mr. Liberty, I am so glad you could join us," said the glowing figure. "I am Arcturus Mengsk, leader of the Sons of Korhal. I would like to ask you to join us."

CHAPTER 7

DEALS

Arcturus Mengsk. There's a name that is synonymous with ter-
ror, betrayal, and violence. A living example of the ends justify-
ing the means. The assassin of the Confederacy of Man. The hero
of the blasted world of Korhal IV. King of the universe. A savage
barbarian who never let anything or anyone get in his way.

And yet, he is also charming, erudite, and intelligent.
When you're in his presence you feel that he's really listen-
ing to you, that your opinions matter, that you're someone
important if you agree with him.

It's amazing. I have often wondered if men like Mengsk
don't carry around their own reality-warping bubbles, and all
who fall in are suddenly transported to another dimension
where the hellish things he says and does suddenly make sense.

At least, that's the effect he always had on me.

—THE LIBERTY MANIFESTO

THE GLOWING FIGURE PAUSED FOR A MOMENT,
then said, "Is there something wrong with our connection, Lieutenant?"

Kerrigan responded, "We read you loud and clear, sir."

"Mr. Liberty, can you hear me?" Arcturus asked.

"I can hear you," said Mike. "I just don't know I can believe what I'm hearing. You're the most hated man in the Confederacy."

Arcturus Mengsk chuckled and folded his hands over his broad, muscle-flat belly. "You honor me, but I must reply that I am only the most hated man among the Confederacy's elites. Those elites who make it their mission to keep everyone else under their thumbs. Those who choose to think otherwise are cast out. I have survived that casting out, and as such I am a danger to them."

Mengsk's words washed over Michael Liberty like warm honey. The man's manner and voice screamed "politician" at every turn. Here was a creature who would be at home in the Tarsonis City Council, or among the confabs and social retreats of the Old Families of the Confederacy.

"I know a lot of reporters who would like to talk to you," Mike said.

"You among them, I hope? I've been a fan of your work for many years. I must admit my surprise at seeing your illustrious name attached to mere military reporting."

Mike shrugged. "There were extenuating circumstances."

"Of course," said Mengsk, another smile appearing beneath his bushy salt-and-pepper mustache. "And similarly, I fear my own vagabond lifestyle has prevented a suitable interview from being set up. The few that have been managed were quickly spoiled by the Confederacy. I think you understand what I mean."

Mike thought of Rourke, dying with Mike's press tags, and of Raynor's people, locked up in orbit, and the refugees waiting for dropships that didn't seem to be appearing. He nodded.

"I know my reputation precedes me, Michael." Mengsk brought himself up short. "May I call you Michael?"

"If you want to."

Another half-concealed smile. "And I must tell you that this reputation is fully deserved. I am, by Confederate lights, a terrorist, an agent of chaos against the old order. My father was Angus Mengsk, who first led the people of Korhal IV in rebellion against the Confederacy."

"And paid for it with the death of the planet."

Arcturus Mengsk turned somber. "Yes, and I carry their ghosts with me every day of my life. They were branded rebels and revolutionaries by the Confederates, but, as you well know, it is the victors who are given the luxury of writing the histories."

Mengsk paused for a moment, but Mike didn't leap in, either to agree or disagree. At length Mengsk said, "I make no apologies for the actions of the Sons of Korhal. There is blood on my hands for my actions, but I have yet to reach the 35 million lives that the Confederacy claimed on Korhal IV."

"Is that a target number?" Mike asked, looking for a chink in the politician's armor.

He expected a flash of anger, or a quick rebuttal. Instead, Mengsk gave a brief chortle. "No. I cannot hope to compete with the merciless bureaucracy of the Confederacy of Man. They wave the banners of Old Earth, but no ancient government would have tolerated the inhumanity that the Confederacy considers business as usual. And those who would raise the alarm are either silenced by violence or shamed into complicity through comfort."

"That would be us in the press," stated Mike, thinking of Handy Anderson's nosebleed office.

Arcturus Mengsk shrugged. "The shoe very well may fit, though I will not press the point. I know that you, for one, are a rare individual who has not shrunk from always seeking the truth."

"So, all this"—Mike waved at the equipment and Kerrigan—"is to set up an interview opportunity?"

Again the easy laugh. "There will be time for interviews later, but there are more pressing matters at the moment. You know the refugee situation in the hinterlands?"

Mike nodded. "I've visited a few of them. They've emptied the cities, and the people are now waiting in the wilderness for the Confederacy dropships to come for them."

"And what would you say if I told you there would be no such ships coming?"

Mike blinked, suddenly aware that Kerrigan was looking at him. "I'd have a hard time believing that. They may be delayed, but they wouldn't abandon the populace here."

"Its true, I'm afraid." Mengsk sighed. Mike wished for some long-distance telepathy himself to dig underneath the man's well-mannered outer mantle. "None are en route. Indeed, Colonel Duke has been very busy for the past few days uprooting the Confederate military structure here, preparing to retreat at the first appearance of the Protoss, or the overwhelming success of the Zerg."

"What do *you* know about the Protoss and the Zerg?" Michael asked sharply.

"More than I want to admit," Mengsk said with a grim smile. "Suffice it to say that they are ancient races, and that they hate each other. And they have little or no use for the human race, either. In that way they are very much like the Confederacy."

"I've seen both the Zerg and the Protoss at work," Mike said. "I have a hard time believing that they are like anything human."

"Even though the Confederacy plans to abandon the population of Mar Sara? To let the Zerg overrun them from below, or the Protoss vaporize them from above? This system is nothing more than a giant petri dish to the bureaucrats on Tarsonis, where they can watch these alien races duel and plan how to save their own hides. Can you, as a man, stand aside and watch this happen?"

Mike thought of the deadly, radiant rainbows on the surface of Chau Sara. "You have a solution," he said, making the words a statement, not a question. "And this solution somehow involves me."

"I am a man with great but not unlimited resources," said Arcturus Mengsk, suddenly with the intensity of a gathering storm. "I have my own ships en route to ferry as many people as I can out of the system. Kerrigan has located the bulk of the camps and spread sufficient anti-Confederate ideas that we may be welcomed as heroes. I have been in contact with the fragments of this planet's government. But I need a friendly face to reassure them that we do indeed come in peace."

"And that's where I come in."

"That's where you come in," Mengsk repeated. "Your reputation precedes you as well."

Mike thought about it, conscious of both the Protoss above and the Zergs below. "I won't fashion propaganda for you," he said at last.

"I'm not asking you to do so," said Mengsk, spreading his hands wide. Welcoming him.

"And I report what I see."

"Which is more than the Confederacy allows you now, under their military strictures. I would expect no less from a reporter of your caliber."

Another pause. Mengsk ended it by saying, "If there's anything I can do to help you further . . ."

Mike thought of Raynor's men. "I have some . . . associates . . . in Confederate custody."

Mengsk raised an eyebrow at Kerrigan. She said, "Local militia and law enforcement officers, sir. They were captured and secured in a prison ship. I can find the location."

"Hmmm. Ask no small favors, eh, Michael?" Mengsk scratched his chin, but even over the connection, Mike knew the man had already made up his mind. "All right, but you have to help with it. But first . . ."

"I know," Mike said with a shrug. "I have to write your bloody press release."

"Exactly," confirmed Mengsk, his eyes twinkling. "If we're agreed, then I'll let Lieutenant Kerrigan take care of the details."

And with that the light-wrapped figure evaporated.

Mike let out a deep breath. "You still reading my mind?" he asked at last.

"It's hard not to," Kerrigan said levelly.

"Then you know I don't trust him."

"I know," answered Mengsk's lieutenant. "But you trust that he'll live up to his side of the bargain. Come on, let's get started."

The prison ship *Merrimack* was an old relic, a *Leviathan*-class battlecruiser that had been stripped of everything useful, save for life support, and even that was quirky and unreliable. Even its drive had been disengaged once it had warped in, and it had been towed to its station high above Mar Sara's northern pole. Its holds were filled with unarmed men, prisoners who had been seized for various reasons and who were considered too dangerous to leave on the surface. There were a lot of the homegrown planetary militia up here, along with the marshals and not a few outspoken local leaders.

What the collection of prisoners, stashed away behind locked bulkheads, did not know was that they were being overseen by a skeleton crew, a fraction of the normal staff of such a prison hulk. Most of the important ranking officers had already been shuttled off, and of the major ships that had visited Mar Sara in the past few days, only the *Norad II* still remained in orbit.

Captain Elias Tudbury, the remaining ranking officer on board the *Merrimack*, growled as he scanned the docking ring monitors. The last shuttle was overdue by at least an hour, and if the radio scuttlebutt was correct, the Protoss with their lightning weapons were due any time now.

And Captain Tudbury had not survived long enough to command a prison ship by exposing himself to danger of any stripe. Now, as the shuttle edged its way toward the dock, he shifted uneasily from one foot to the other. Beside him the comm officer was monitoring frequencies.

The sooner the shuttle arrived, Tudbury thought, the sooner he and his few stragglers could get away from here, leaving the prisoners to their fate.

The speaker crackled over his head. "Prison Shu . . . port five-four . . . requ . . . sting clear . . . for docking. Passphrase . . ." The rest was lost in static.

The comm officer tapped his headpiece and said, "Repeat transmission, five-four-six-seven. I say again, repeat transmission."

The speaker continued to crack and spark. ". . . ison shuttle . . . six-seven. Requesting clearance . . . king. Pass . . ." More static.

"Come again, five-four-six-seven," said the comm officer. Tudbury was practically exploding with anxiety, but the comm officer's voice was soft and mechanical. "Please repeat."

"Interferen . . ." came the response. "We wi . . . pull off and tr . . . gain later."

"No you don't," said Tudbury, reaching past his officer and flicking a switch. "Shuttle five-four-six-seven, ya'll are cleared for docking. Get your ass in here and get us off this tub!"

The hydraulics hissed as the two ships linked, while the communications officer pointed out the violation of standard protocol.

"This is a nonstandard situation, son," said Tudbury, already halfway to the dock, his duffel already packed and swinging behind him. "Grab your gear and spread the word. We're off this here wreck!"

The airlock slid open, and Captain Tudbury was looking down the barrel of a large-bore slugthrower. At the operating end of the slugthrower was a lean man with a ponytail who looked like someone Tudbury had seen on UNN.

"Boo," said Michael Liberty.

It took a mere ten minutes to overpower the rest of the crew, most of whom were armed only with their duffels and a great desire to leave, and another twenty to convince them to reengage the warp engines and limp the *Merrimack* out of planetary range. Raynor and his men took the shuttle with Liberty.

"I'll admit," said former marshal Raynor, "that when I told you to do something, I didn't expect this."

Mike Liberty blushed. "Let's just say I made a deal with the devil, and it worked out to our benefit."

As if on cue, Mengsk's broad face filled the shuttle's viewscreen. "Congratulations, Michael. We must report success as well with our endeavor. We have been welcomed with open arms by the people of Mar Sara and even now our ships are evacuating the refugees. I have come to understand that even Colonel Duke is unwilling to fire on ships filled with innocents, and the turn of events has vexed him dearly."

Raynor leaned toward the screen. "Mengsk? This is Jim Raynor. I just want to thank you for your help in getting us off that hulk."

"Ah, Marshal Raynor. Michael apparently thinks very highly of you and your men. I was wondering if you would be willing to help me in a small matter." Mengsk's smile filled the screen

"Now wait a minute, Mengsk," said Mike. "We made a deal here, and we both did our part."

"And that bargain is done, Michael," continued the terrorist leader who had saved the population of a planet. "But now I want to offer a similar arrangement to the former marshal and his men. Something that, I hope, will be beneficial to *all* our peoples."

CHAPTER 8

ZERG AND PROTOSS

It would be easy to declare that Arcturus Mengsk was a master manipulator, which he was, or that he regularly deceived others, which was true as well. But it would be a mistake to deny all personal responsibility in falling into his web.

It seems now the height of folly ever to have dealt with the man, but think of the situation when the Sara system died. You had the mindless beasts of the Zerg on one side, and the unholy fury of the Protoss on the other. And in the middle you had the criminal bureaucracy of the old Confederacy of Man, which was willing to write off the population of two planets in order to learn more about its enemies.

With such a surplus of devils in the universe, what did it matter if there was one more?

—THE LIBERTY MANIFESTO

THE JACOBS INSTALLATION WAS BUILT INTO THE side of a mountain on the far side of Mar Sara from its major cities. It wasn't listed in any planetary archive that Michael Liberty had found, but Mengsk knew about it.

Somewhere in the Jacobs Installation there was a computer with data in it. Mengsk said he didn't know what the data was, but he knew it was important. And he knew that he needed it. And he knew that Raynor would go get it for him.

All of this made Mike wonder what else Mengsk knew. It also made the reporter think about other deep craters on Chau Sara. Had there been similar locations on the other planet, unknown to most humans but beacons to the Protoss? Had Mengsk known about these as well?

Liberty suddenly felt as though he were at the epicenter of a bomb site, and the countdown had already begun.

The planet was already unraveling. He could see the devastation from the screens on the dropship that brought Raynor and his combat troops in. Miles of former farmland was now overrun with the creep, a pulsing living organism that covered the earth and sent tendrils deep into the rock beneath. Odd constructs dotted the landscape like twisted mushrooms, and scorpion-like creatures pulled down and consumed anything in their path. He could see packs of the skinned-dog zerglings, herded by the larger snake-beast hydralisks. And once, on the horizon, there was a flight of things that looked like winged organic cannons.

The creep had not reached the Jacobs Installation yet, but the strange Zerg towers were already on the horizon. The front gates were open, and men were trying to flee the complex. The dropship came under fire as it deployed Raynor and his troops. Even in the relative safety of a low-grade technician's combat suit, Liberty hung back.

I'm not doing this for Mengsk, he told himself. *I'm doing it for Raynor.*

The guards were more interested in flight than fight, and Raynor's troops scattered them easily. Michael Liberty followed the hulking armored forms into the base itself.

The resistance stiffened as soon as they entered. Defensive guns were mounted in the wall, and popup turrets erupted at every corner. Raynor lost two men before he got cautious.

"We need to find some control computer," said Mike.

"Yeah," Raynor agreed. "But I'm willing to bet it's on the *far* side of those guns."

And with that he was out in the corridor, spraying spikes in a wide arc, hitting targets that had been unseen a moment ago. Mike followed as close as he dared, his own gauss rifle at the ready, but by the time he rounded the corner Raynor was standing in a smoking hallway. Charred emplacements scorched the walls and floor.

Another hundred feet and another intersection. And another turret popping up from the floor like a mechanical gopher, spraying the hallway.

Raynor and Liberty dodged into one doorway, three others of the squad into another. One man wasn't fast enough and was caught in the stream of bullets, his fall forward slowed by the continual impacts of the spikes against his helmet and shattered chest plate.

"Okay, we need to take this one out," said Raynor.

"Hold on," said Mike. "I think I found something."

It looked akin to a typical comm center, with zooming screens on either side and altogether too many buttons. But the screens showed what looked like a diagram of the installation itself.

"It's a map," said Raynor.

"Full marks," said Mike. "Better yet, it's a map that we can use."

Several areas already flashed red, marking where the assault team had already passed. Other regions were flashing green pips, including the one outside the door. Probably active defenses.

"Right," said Mike. "You know anything about computers?"

"Had to replace a memory board on my Vulture once," said Raynor.

"Dandy." Mike's own experience consisted of repairing persnickety comm units in the field, but he didn't say anything. He scanned the various buttons and toggles. All were numbered, but there was no master listing.

He hit a toggle, and one of the green lights went out. He hit another and another vanished. He started flipping the toggles and mashing the buttons wildly. About fifteen seconds later the staccato in the hallway stopped.

"Nice job," said Raynor.

"Let's see what the others do." Mike grabbed a small dial and turned it. Somewhere deep in the complex a Klaxon sounded, and there was a vibration under their feet.

"What the Sam Hill was that?" said Raynor.

"The sound of me pushing my luck too far," said Mike.

"So why did you do that?"

"It seemed like the right thing to do at the time."

Raynor let out a frustrated sigh, then said, "Can you get the data we're looking for off this terminal?"

Mike shook his head, running a finger over the installation schematic. "Here," he said. "There's a separate system, not linked up to the mainframe."

"Think that's it?"

"Has to be. The best way to protect information from hackers is to completely separate the machine that it's on. Basic computer security one-oh-one."

"Then let's go whack some varmints," said Raynor, signaling to the survivors of the squad.

"Yeah," Mike said with a laugh. "Let's git them 'varmints.'"

They stepped out, then dodged back immediately as another volley of spikes ricocheted down the hallway.

"Liberty!" Raynor bellowed. "I thought you got all the gun emplacements!"

"Those aren't emplacements, Jim," Mike shouted back, squatting in the doorway. "Those are live targets."

Indeed, there was a pair of white-armored forms

now at the crossroads, their combat armor similar to Mike's own save for color. They carried their own gauss rifles and were spraying the corridor.

Mike brought his own weapon up and leaned forward for a shot. A white-armored specter hovered in his crosshairs.

And Mike found he could not shoot. His target was a man, a living human. He could not shoot.

The target in white armor harbored no such compunctions, and let loose a burst. The door frame splintered under the assault as Liberty rolled back into the room.

"What happened?" Raynor shouted. "They in cover?"

"They . . ." Mike began, then shook his head. "I can't shoot them."

Raynor frowned. "You took out a Zerg with a shotgun. I saw you."

"That was different. These are humans."

Mike expected the admission to disgust the lawman, but instead Raynor merely nodded and said, "That's okay. Lots of folks have a problem with shooting other people. The good news is that *they* don't know you don't want to shoot them. Fire a little over their heads. That will spook 'em."

He pushed Mike back toward the door. Across the hallway the other two marines were trading shots with the white-armored forms.

Mike rolled out of the doorway, targeted the one on the right, raised his gauss rifle just a hair, and let off a burst. The white form dropped into a crouch, while his companion brought his own weapon around and dropped to one knee.

Despite himself, Mike smiled. Then the chest of the soldier he had fired above blossomed in a fountain of blood. His companion brought his own weapon around, but too slowly. His head vaporized in a red mist as visor and helmet shattered.

Mike looked up to see Raynor standing above him, leaning out of the doorway. He had taken the two enemy troopers out with single shots.

Raynor looked down and said, "I understand if you have a problem shooting people. Fortunately, I don't. Now let's go."

The wall and floor guns were silent now, and the team was practically running through the halls. In his lighter armor, Mike was in front.

He suddenly realized that this was not the smartest place to be.

Then he rounded the corner and sprawled over a zergling.

In one graceless swoop Mike skidded forward, tumbling over the top of the skinless beast. He could feel the creature's muscles pulse and shudder beneath him as he inadvertently vaulted over it. He landed on his shoulder and felt pain ratchet through the right side of his body.

"Zerg!" Mike shouted. "Kill it!" He ignored the pain and twisted his rifle around, praying it hadn't been damaged in the fall.

"Crossfire!" Raynor bellowed. "We'll hit each other!"

There was a silent moment in the hallway—Raynor's troops on one side, Mike on the other, the Zerg in the middle. This close, Mike could smell the creature's fetid breath. Its very skin seemed to exude decay and rot.

The zergling turned toward the squad, then toward the reporter, as if trying to determine which to attack first. Finally some organic circuit closed in its twisted mind and it came to its decision.

It leapt at Liberty with a chittering cry, its claws extended.

Mike dove forward, underneath the leap, and raised his gauss rifle. He caught the creature in the belly, spearing it and catching the beast's own momentum. Beast and barrel rose in a slow arc above him.

At the top of the arc Mike pulled the trigger, and a volley of spikes splattered the zergling. Those that passed through its body embedded in the metal ceiling of the hallway.

Mike sputtered as he was drenched in the beast's ichor. Raynor ran up.

"What are Zerg doing here?" Raynor asked.

"Maybe they're after what we're after?" Mike suggested.

"Let's find that information, now." Raynor waved the remains of the team forward.

"Let's find a shower," Mike muttered, wiping the Zerg's guts off his stained armor.

The complex had a few surprises left. The passage widened into a larger room. Three more zerglings were within, brought down in rapid fire before they could react. Along one wall was a line of cages, all open. They gave off the fetid smell of the zerglings.

"They were keeping them here," said Raynor. "Pets? Studies?"

"And for how long?" Mike reached the isolated computer station and started hitting buttons. "Christ. Look at this."

"The information?"

"That, and more. Look at this. These are readings on the Zerg going back months."

"But that's impossible," said Raynor. "Unless . . ."

"Unless the Confederates knew about the Zerg all the time. They knew they were here. Hell, they may have *brought* them here."

"Samuel J. Houston on a bicycle," said Raynor. Mike assumed that was a curse. Then Raynor added, "Get the disk and let's move out."

"Working," said Mike. The disk burner chugged for a few minutes, then ejected a silvery wafer. "Got it. Let's go!"

The moment Mike plucked the disk from the machine, the lighting suddenly went red. From above them a female voice intoned, "Self-destruct sequence initiated."

"Crap!" cursed Mike. "It must have been booby-trapped!"

"Let's move!" said Raynor. "Don't make any wrong turns!"

Mike, in his lighter armor, led, now unafraid of running into any other surprises. They encountered nothing but the dead on their way out, the soft tones above them warning them, "Ten seconds to detonation," then "Five seconds to detonation."

Then they were outside, beneath the rotten-orange sky. Mike kept running, intending not to stop until he reached the dropship.

Raynor caught up with him and threw him to the ground.

Mike bellowed a curse at the marshal, but it was drowned out by the explosion.

The entire side of the mountain rippled from the detonation, focusing a single blast from the mouth of the installation. A blistering hot wave washed over Liberty and the prostrate marines, and the top of the mountain fell in on itself. Mike hugged the bucking earth and prayed. And once it stopped, he realized that if he had been standing, he would have been blown away in the blast.

"Thanks," he said to Raynor.

"Seemed like the right thing to do at the time," said the former lawman. "Come on, let's get back before the Zerg find us here."

Mengsk was waiting for them on the bridge of his own command ship, the *Hyperion*. Compared to the bridge of the *Norad II*, this bridge was smaller and cozier, more of a den/library than the nerve center of a fleet. The perimeter of the room was dotted by technicians speaking softly into comm units. A large screen dominated one wall.

Of Lieutenant Kerrigan, Mike noticed, there was no sign.

"There were Zerg there!" said Raynor, handing over the disk. "The Confederates have been studying the damned aliens for months!"

"Years," said Mengsk, unsurprised. "I saw Zerg in Confederate holding pens myself, and that was over a year ago. It's clear the Confederates have known of these creatures for some time. For all we know, they could be *breeding* them."

Mike said nothing. The bottom had dropped out of the Confederate secrets market. There was nothing that they did that would surprise him now.

Raynor's jaw dropped open. "You mean, they've been using my planet as some sort of laboratory for these . . . things?"

"Your planet and your sister world," said Mengsk. "And gods know how many more Fringe Worlds. They've sowed the wind, my friends, and now they are reaping the whirlwind."

For the first time, Raynor was stopped in his tracks. The enormity of the crime, Mike thought, was just too much for his local law-enforcement brain. Who do you arrest when the crime is genocide? How do you punish for such crimes?

Mike spoke up. "I've got a report to file. Summarizes everything we've found so far."

"We have a scrambled comm setup for your use,"

said Mengsk. "But you know they'll never run the story."

"I have to take that chance," Mike admitted, but inwardly he had to agree with Mengsk. If the Old Families of Tarsonis were paranoid enough to threaten a scandalmonger like him over a construction scandal, how willing were they to admit to dealing with planet-devouring aliens?

Mike was suddenly glad that the mind reader wasn't present.

A soft bell chimed, and one of the technicians announced, "We're getting warp signatures at mark four-point-five-point-seven.

"Pull back to a safe distance, scan on maximum," said Mengsk. "Gentlemen, you may remain if you want to see the last act of this particularly tawdry passion play."

Neither Mike nor Raynor moved, and Mengsk turned back to the screen. The huge orange ball of Mar Sara loomed over them, a few white clouds scattered high across its northern hemisphere. Yet most of that orange surface was now mottled, spoiled. Overrun by the creep, and the things that lived in it.

The very surface of the land seemed to pulsate and bubble, heaving like a living thing. The creep had even spread over the oceans in broad mats, writhing like living carpets of algae.

There was nothing human left on the planet. Not alive, at any rate.

A flash blossomed to one side of the planetary disk,

and Mike knew that the Protoss had arrived. Their lightning ships warped into being. A flash of blue-white electricity, and then they were there. The golden carriers with their moth attendants, and metallic bat-winged creations that wove among the larger ships. They were breathtaking and deadly, forces of war raised to the level of an art form.

Mengsk spoke softly into his throat mike, and Mike could feel the engines engage. The terrorist leader was prepared to get out at the first sign that the Protoss had noticed them.

He need not have worried. The Protoss were completely intent on the diseased planet beneath them. Hatchways opened up in the bottoms of the larger ships, and great beams of energy, so intense as to be colorless, lanced downward toward the surface. The aliens laid down a withering barrage against the planet beneath.

Where the energy beams struck, they burned. The sky itself curdled as the beams pierced through the atmospheric envelope. Air itself was torn away from the planet by the force of the blows.

And where the beams struck the surface, they erupted, boiling the ground where they struck, uprooting both the creep-infested lands and those that had not yet been infected. Deadly rainbow radiation, more brilliant than Mike had ever seen, spiraled out from the impact points, churning earth and water mercilessly, distorting the matter of the planet itself.

Then other ships began firing thinner beams with

surgical accuracy, adding to the barrage in places. The cities, Mike realized. They were targeting the cities and making sure that nothing could survive there. Any place of human settlement. Including, he knew, the Jacobs Installation itself.

They had cut their timing very close indeed, he thought, and his stomach gave an uneasy lurch.

One of the pulsing beams punched through the crust itself, and the ground erupted in a volcanic upwelling. Magma pushed to the surface, consuming everything that had been uprooted by the energy beams. Most of the world's atmosphere was burning now, torn away from the orb in a veil that trailed it in orbit, and what was left spiraled in hurricanes and tornadoes, until destroyed by more beams.

Now red volcanic glows covered the northern hemisphere of Mar Sara like welts. The remainder of the land heaved in a deadly rainbow. Nothing could survive the assault, human or otherwise.

"Exterminators," said Mike softly. "They're cosmic exterminators."

"Indeed," said Mengsk. "And they *can't* or *won't* tell the difference between us and the Zerg. Maybe to them there is no difference. We should prepare for departure. They may notice us at any time."

Mike looked at Raynor. The former marshal was stone-faced and grim, his hands clutching the railing in front of him. In the light of screens that showed the blue lightning of the Protoss ships, he looked like a statue. Only his eyes were alive, and they were filled with infinite sadness.

"Raynor?" said Mike. "Jim? Are you all right?"

"No," said Jim Raynor softly. "I mean, can any of us be all right after this?"

Mike had no response, and sat there as the planet died and Arcturus Mengsk spoke softly into his throat mike. After a moment, the terrorist leader said, "We are ready for departure."

"All right," said Raynor, his eyes never leaving the screen. "Let's go."

CHAPTER 9

MARSHAL AND GHOST

James Raynor was the most decent man I ever encountered during the fall of the Confederacy. Everyone else, I can safely say, was either a victim or a villain, or quite often both.

At first wash, Raynor seems like a backwoods cowboy, one of those good old boys that you see in the bars swapping lies about the days gone by. There's a cocksureness, an overconfidence about him that just makes you bridle initially. Yet over time you come to see him as a valuable ally and—dare I say it?—a friend.

It all comes from belief. Jim Raynor believed in himself, and he believed in those around him. And from that belief came the strength that allowed him and those who followed him to survive everything else the universe threw at him.

Jim Raynor was a most decent and honorable man. I suppose that's why his is the greatest tragedy of this godforsaken war.

—THE LIBERTY MANIFESTO

MENGSK STRUCK LIBERTY AS JUST ANOTHER politician. For all the ghosts that supposedly haunted the man, his motivations were as apparent as those of the lowest ward heeler on Tarsonis. He was still gathering his power, and unwilling to pass on any potential ally. It was, Mike realized, why he knew the man would keep his word—he was still in a position where it would be dangerous for him if it got around that he did not.

Mengsk made Raynor a captain for his troubles, and Liberty was granted a series of one-on-one interviews. Mike avoided the level of propaganda that Mengsk apparently desired, but that made the charismatic leader even more available to Mike's questions. Mike's own resistance made his approval more desirable to the rebel commander.

Slowly, Mike found himself agreeing more and more with Mengsk's opinions of the Confederates. Hell, he himself had said many of the same things, though in a more cautious fashion, in various reports over the years. The Confederacy of Man was a criminal bureaucracy, filled to the brim with career politicos and grafters whose battle cry was "Where's Mine?"

And Mengsk was right about another matter. UNN never ran anything of his report on the destruction of Mar Sara, or of the Confederate culpability in the attack. They did get around to telling the people that there was not one but two hostile enemy threats out in the universe, the subversive Zerg and the sky-blasting Protoss. Both were presented as implacable foes of humanity, and the only solution was to group together beneath the Confederate flag to repulse them.

"Such is the nature of tyrants," said Mengsk late one evening on the *Hyperion*'s observation deck, his snifter of brandy untouched on the table between them. Liberty's glass had long since been drained and set down empty beside a chess set of which the white king had been toppled. Mengsk played black as habit, Liberty usually lost as white. An unused ashtray rested at the far end of the table. Michael had given up smoking again, but Mengsk made it available to him nonetheless.

Mengsk continued, "Tyrants can only survive by presenting a greater tyrant as a threat. The Confederacy does not realize the danger of the other tyrants that it has now called down upon all of us."

"Before the Protoss and Zerg," Mike noted, "their favorite threat was *you.*"

Mengsk chuckled. "I must admit that I feel that the best form of government is benevolent despotism. I don't think the oligarchs in charge agree with that."

"And are *you* pointing at greater tyrants to cover your own abuses?" Mike asked.

"Of course I am," said Arcturus Mengsk. "But it does help that our foes *are* greater tyrants than we are. Or ever intend to be." He picked up Mike's toppled king from the board. "Another game, perhaps?"

Mike saw nothing of Kerrigan, and when asked,

Mengsk only said, "My trusted lieutenant works best in the field." Mike took that to mean that she was out sizing up another planet ripe for rebellion.

He was right. Two days later Mengsk called both Liberty and Raynor to his observation deck. A graphic display showed another world, this one a ruddy brown. Behind it a gas giant loomed like an overprotective parent.

"Antiga Prime," said Mengsk, tapping the screen. "Border colony of the Confederacy of Man. Its people are very, very tired of the Confederate military, which has gotten a bit heavy-handed since the Protoss and Zerg first appeared. I want Captain Raynor to help the Antigans get their revolt off the ground. That means dealing with a unit of Alpha Squadron they've got baby-sitting the major road on the ground."

"My pleasure, sir," said Raynor. Mike noted that Raynor seemed calmer, more controlled now than he had when they left the Sara system. Incorporating his own unit's survivors with Mengsk's Sons of Korhal apparently helped see him through the loss of Mar Sara, and his bold, brazen nature was bubbling once more to the surface. He was itching for action.

Mengsk turned. "And Mr. Liberty, if you want to accompany his unit?"

"You may have overlooked this fact, Arcturus," said Liberty, "but I'm still not working for you."

"You're not working for anyone at the moment, it seems," replied Mengsk. "The UNN has been noticeably devoid of your illustrious presence. I only thought you would be professionally interested . . ."

"And . . . ?" prompted Liberty.

"And your glib tongue and clever notepad might be enough to encourage the Antigans to cast off their shackles." He smiled a slightly shamefaced grin, and Mike knew that he was going planetside.

Antiga Prime had once been a water world, but the oceans had left without leaving a forwarding address. All that remained were hard mudflats and low, flat mesas covered with a native shrub with purple blossoms. Occasionally the whitened bones of some fossilized sea creatures rippled out of the surrounding strata, the only reminder that life larger than humans had once been here. Pretty in an arid, lifeless sort of way.

The dropship brought them down on a low plateau that looked like every other low plateau on Antiga.

Mengsk had mentioned that his scout would contact them once they were on the ground. Mike had no doubt who that scout would be. As the rebels set up a perimeter around the ship, he kept the comm link open to Mengsk and the regional commanders.

Kerrigan appeared out of nowhere, despite the fact that there was no cover around. She was dressed in ghost armor—a hostile environment suit—and had a canister rifle slung across her back. Her helmet was off, and her red hair flashed in Antiga's too-bright sun.

Kerrigan snapped off a quick salute. "Captain

Raynor, I've finished scouting out the area and . . .
You pig!"

Mike quickly turned down the volume on his
comm unit. Raynor lurched backward as if struck.

"What?" he said. "I haven't even said anything to
you yet!"

Kerrigan's too-wide lips turned into a nasty sneer.
"Yeah, but you were *thinking* it."

"Oh yeah, you're a telepath," said Raynor, shooting
Mike a look that even the reporter could read. *And
why didn't you warn me about this?* To the lieutenant he
said, "Look, let's just get on with this, okay?"

Kerrigan snorted. "Right. The command center is a
couple klicks due west, up on one of those mesas.
Alpha Squad, but no Duke. Sorry, boys. We take them
out, and the indigenous forces would be willing to rise
in rebellion. There are some towers that need to come
down if I'm to get in."

"Right," said Raynor, frowning. "I don't *need* to tell
you to move out."

"No, you don't," said Kerrigan, a touch too hotly.
"But there's another thing."

"Go ahead, Lieutenant," said Raynor. "I *don't* read
minds."

"There have been increasing reports of xenomorphs in the area." Kerrigan almost smiled at the
reaction to her words.

Raynor frowned deeply.

Mike nearly jumped in his seat. "Xenomorphs?
Zerg? Here?"

"Cattle mutilations, mysterious disappearances, bug-eyed monsters," confirmed Kerrigan. "The usual suspects. Not a lot, but enough."

"Crap," muttered Raynor. "Confederates *and* Zerg. They seem to go hand in hand. Okay, *now* let's roll out."

The wide, dried mudflats of Antiga Prime were ideal for speed and lousy for cover. Twice marine scouts appeared to the south, distracting Raynor in his Vulture to deal with them as Kerrigan, Raynor's troops, and Mike slowly crept up on the mesa. They were about three hundred yards shy when a tower cannon opened up on them.

Mike's comm link crackled. "Dammit," said Kerrigan. "They've got sensors out the buttcheeks on that thing. I can't even sneeze without it picking me up. Can you get reinforcements on that blower?"

"Working on it," snapped Mike as another shell bounded into the outcropping above him. "Raynor! It's Liberty! We're pinned down! Need your firepower, *muy pronto.*"

Mike was unsure that the former marshal had gotten the message, until he heard the high-pitched whine of Raynor's Vulture engines. The captain topped a nearby rise in a single hop, closing as the tower tried to traverse its gun to the new target. It was too slow, and with a resounding thump a volley of frag grenades shot from under the vehicle's front hood. Blossoms of flame erupted at the base of the tower.

Kerrigan gave a cry, and the remaining pinned troops rolled out of their hiding places and lacerated the tower with spike fire. Raynor passed for another blitz, but it was overkill: by the time a second string of explosions blossomed at the base, the tower was already listing, and as Raynor sped off, it toppled completely in his wake.

Mike's private line crackled. "Next time, make it something important, buddy!" said the captain.

"What did he say?" Kerrigan asked, then added, "Never mind. He's a pig, but he's a pretty competent pig."

Mike shook his head. "Captain Raynor is one of the most upright, moral men I've met since leaving Tarsonis."

"Yeah, he's that way on the surface," said Kerrigan. "Everything's under real tight control. It's underneath that he's a pig, like most people. Trust me on this."

Mike didn't know what to say. Eventually he managed, "He has been under a lot of stress lately."

Kerrigan snorted again. "Yeah, like who hasn't?"

They were within sight of the command center, another standard-issue half sphere, a portable setup. This one glistened in the sun, though: the Zerg hadn't corrupted it yet. Somehow that made Mike feel both better and worse at the same time.

Another call came in. This time Raynor was looking for reinforcements. Could Kerrigan send down the troops still with her?

"He says—" Mike began.

"Send them," said Kerrigan.

"But you've got to—"

"I've got to get inside. And I can do that either with or without the support troops. They're just extra targets. Send them off, and follow when you can."

Mike relayed the orders, while Kerrigan put up the hood and helmet of her ghost suit. Mike watched her fasten the helmet, touch a device at her belt, and . . .

Vanish.

No, not quite vanish. There was a ripple around her, one that you could follow if you knew what to look for, and looked very hard. The guards at the front of the command center did not know what to look for, and were not looking hard enough. There was a burst of unseen canister fire, and the guards blew apart in a couple pieces each. Then an explosion at the main gates, which suddenly yawned wide. There was a silhouette among the smoke for a moment, a female figure with a large gun. Then she was gone, into the depths of the enemy command center.

Mike followed slowly, very much aware that he lacked the cloaking technology and psionic talent that made the telepathic ghosts possible. He paused briefly near the dead guards. They wore Alpha Squadron uniforms, but their bleeding heads were covered with helmets polarized in the Antigan sunlight. He decided not to remove the helmets: these might be people he knew. People who still owed him poker money.

Mike sneaked into the devastation of the command center.

It was easy to know where Kerrigan had gone; Mike just followed the path of broken and bleeding corpses. Men and women in full combat rig had been tossed around like rag dolls and now lay crumpled in pools of their own blood.

Michael Liberty thought briefly of Lieutenant Swallow and realized that he was now getting used to freshly dead bodies. Maybe he was growing the necessary emotional armor to survive in a universe at war.

He found Kerrigan's canister rifle, rammed through the front plexishield of a toppled Goliath walker. From up ahead came the sounds of battle. Despite himself, he cradled his own gauss rifle and pressed forward.

And he was rewarded with the privilege of watching Sarah Kerrigan fight.

It was blood poetry, war ballet. She had reached the center of the command center now, armed with her knife and a slugthrower. She would wink into existence, slit a throat, then wink out again. Marines would rush to that location, and she would appear a few feet away, firing a burst point-blank into the helmet of her target. Then gone, then back again, this time with a spinning kick that broke the neck of a bellowing officer.

Mike brought his weapon up but found he could

not fire. It was more than just a reluctance to take human life. He could not tell where she was at any one time. And through it all she moved with a cat-like grace and determination that shredded every opponent she encountered.

She *was* very good with knives. More important, she was like the Protoss—glorious and deadly.

He stood in the entrance for only a minute, but it was enough time for Kerrigan to dispatch every enemy in the command center. The only survivors were the ones who chose to flee at the outset.

Only then did Kerrigan come fully into view, sinking to her knees in exhaustion, her back to Liberty.

Mike walked up behind her and moved to put his hand on her shoulder.

His hand never reached her. Without hesitation, she spun in place, grabbed his outstretched wrist with one hand, and brought up her combat knife with the other.

Only when the tip of the knife was inches from Mike's face did she freeze. Her face was a mask of rage. Fear flooded Mike's mind, and in an instant he knew she was aware of that fear.

"Don't. *Do.* That," she said, biting off each word. Then she dropped her knife and put her face in both hands, "You're afraid of me."

Mike hesitated for a moment, then settled on "You betcha."

"I'm sorry," she said. "Sorry you had to see this."

Mike took a deep breath. "I just never visited you

at work before. You rest for a moment. I've got to kick off a revolution."

He shoved a broken body from the communications console, inserted the prerecorded disk, set the levels, and put out a general signal on all bands.

"This is Michael Liberty, broadcasting from Antiga Prime, with a report that the master command center for this world has been disabled by rebel forces. Repeat, the master command center has been disabled. The power of the Confederacy has been interrupted, and there is a strong possibility that it can be shattered entirely if the people of Antiga rise up to take control of their own destiny. The Confederate Marines in charge of the command center are either dead or in full retreat, while rebel losses have been . . ." He looked at Sarah Kerrigan, exhausted, weeping into her hands. ". . . been minimal. We have a message here from Arcturus Mengsk, leader of the Sons of Korhal. Please stand by."

Mike popped the preprogrammed cartridge into the player and let the smooth, melodious tones of the terrorist leader rouse the people to action. Mike went back to Kerrigan, this time circling her so she knew he was coming.

Her eyes were dry now, but she was shuddering, her arms crossed in front of her, her breathing in short gasps.

"Its okay," said Mike. "You got them all."

"I know," she said, looking at Mike. "I got them all. And as I killed each and every one of them, I knew what they were thinking. Fear. Panic. Hatred. Hopelessness. Breakfast."

"Breakfast?"

"One of the techs had skipped breakfast, and he was really regretting not having had waffles." Kerrigan gave a sniffling giggle. "He was about to have his throat slit, and he was worrying about waffles." She put her hands along the sides of her head and ran her fingers through her red hair. "It sucks being a telepath."

"I'll bet," said Mike, aware that the fear was still with him. The fear that Kerrigan could cut open his belly before he could even react. And that she knew he was thinking that.

"I know you're afraid," said Kerrigan. "And you can admit it. That makes you smarter than most. God, what I went through to become this, what the Confederates did to me. Do you know?"

"I know that the Confederacy has a lot of deep holes to hide their secrets in. Deeper and blacker than I ever imagined. Ghost training was for an elite group of carefully controlled telepaths . . ."

Kerrigan was nodding as he spoke. "Controlled through drugs and threats and brutality, until they owned you body and soul. They are no better than these Zerg creatures, creating warriors for a larger empire. We have no lives but the ones the Confederacy allows us, until we are no longer useful, and then we are discarded, lest we create future problems. Unless . . ."

"Unless you escape," said Mike. "Or someone helps you escape." And he suddenly realized why this former ghost was working for Arcturus Mengsk. She owed him her life.

Kerrigan just nodded in response. "There's more to it, but yes."

There were heavy footfalls at the entrance, and Mike rose with his gauss rifle ready. Raynor's armored form appeared in the doorway.

"You children okay?" he shouted.

"We're done here," said Mike. "Center captured, message delivered."

"Good," said Captain Raynor, " 'cause we've got a chunk of Alpha Squad coming up from the south, and we're going to need all the help we can get handling them. She okay?"

"I'm fine," said Kerrigan, rising to her feet. "You can talk to me directly, you know."

"Maybe I'll just *think* it at you," said Raynor.

"Jim!" Mike said sharply. "That's enough."

"What?" Raynor looked surprised by Mike's tone.

"That's *enough*," repeated Mike, his tone less heated but still grave. His serious voice.

The large captain looked at Mike, then slowly nodded. "Yeah, I suppose it is." To Kerrigan he said, "Sorry to offend, ma'am."

"Used to it, Captain," said Kerrigan. "You said we had more Confederates to kill. Let's get a move on."

She forced her way past both men, phasing invisible as she went.

Captain Raynor shook his head. "Women."

Mike softened his tone. "She's been under a lot of stress lately."

Raynor snorted. "Could have fooled me."

The pair followed Raynor out of the building. Along the horizon there were small flashes of battle as the Antigans and Confederates met in combat.

Above them, in the darkening sky, there were other flashes, of another battle. They danced across the sky like new stars and ended only when a brilliant meteor streaked across the sky, splitting the screaming atmosphere in its wake.

CHAPTER 10

THE WRECK OF THE *NORAD II*

There's an old Earth word. Its called schadenfreude—*the feeling of elation that comes from learning of the suffering of others. Like when you hear that a rival newsman suddenly was caught cursing in front of a live mike, or that a particularly corrupt alderman just stepped in front of a garbage truck. It's elation accompanied by that twinge of guilt for feeling so good, and the quiet, fervent prayer that something that bad never happens to you.*

With the Protoss and Zerg biting deep into Confederate territory, we had schadenfreude *in buckets.*

—THE LIBERTY MANIFESTO

OTHER MEN AND WOMEN WENT TO WAR. MIKE returned to Mengsk's base and monitored the flow of communications. There was the blind panic he had come to expect during warfare—units suddenly cut off and demanding, then pleading for, reinforcements, then relief and finally rescue. Other messages from units that suddenly evaporated in a haze of radiation.

And still other messages, these from civilians, asking for help from anyone, on any side.

And then there were the anomalous reports, the ones of monsters suddenly appearing in the countryside, ascribed to the Confederates, or the rebels, or to invasions from beyond. These reports were growing more numerous by the hour, and they convinced Mike that Kerrigan was right: the Zerg were on Antiga.

He wanted to hit the console when that realization sank in. Zerg presence was as good as a cancer diagnosis, and much more fatal. Until they figured out how to defeat them, the Zerg would eat this world alive. Or the Protoss—fatal chemotherapy—would sterilize it to keep the Zerg from spreading.

"But it doesn't work that way, does it?" said Mike to the comm unit. "A few cells always seem to escape, and the cancer keeps growing."

The fury he felt in his belly lasted only a moment, then was replaced with amazement as the next message rattled through his earpiece.

"This is General Duke, calling from the Alpha Squadron flagship Norad II! *We've crash-landed and are being hit hard by the Zerg! Request immediate backup from anyone receiving this signal! Repeat, this is a priority one distress call. This is General Duke . . ."*

The distress call went into a loop, and Michael listened to it three more times before checking the other channels.

There were a couple calls asking for confirmation,

and a plethora of other responses, describing attacks by the Zerg and Antigan rebels, and in one case, an assault by other Confederate forces. And there were now reports of Protoss ships in-system, fighting something themselves, probably Zerg similar to the ones that brought down the *Norad II*, out in the outer rim of ice worlds. There were even some reports of Protoss ground forces appearing. There was a lot of noise, but nothing that resembled an honest, solid offer of help.

He's cooked, thought Michael. *Old Duke's goose is finally cooked.*

Raynor stormed in about ten minutes later. "Mike, you're with me. Suit up."

"What's up?" Mike asked, reaching for his combat armor.

"You didn't hear the news in here?" Raynor looked as though lightning bolts would spring from his brow at any moment.

"The normal panic and despair," said Mike, waving at the board. "Oh, yeah. I heard Duke finally got promoted to general. Should we send a fruit basket?"

"Funny, newshound. Mengsk wants us to go in and rescue him. He thinks Duke would make a good ally."

Mike blinked at the captain. "I'm hearing things, right?"

"That's what I said," Raynor said, holding out Mike's helmet.

"He's crazy!"

"It's been noted," Raynor said grimly.

"And Mengsk wants *me* to go? It's news I can cover from here."

"*I* want you to come along. That bastard locked me and my boys up. I'm going to want someone there who he's willing to talk to."

"Did I mention that the last time I talked to him he had me forcibly ejected from his bridge?" said Mike, taking the helmet.

"It's come up, but at least I'm sure you're not going to shoot him right away."

Mike locked down the helmet and followed Raynor out of the comm area. "I suddenly have a craving for a cigarette."

"Maybe you can bum one off Duke."

Only when they were on the road did Mike think to ask, "Does Kerrigan know about this?"

"Uh-huh."

"And she thinks it's a good idea?"

"Actually," said the former lawman, "she's the one who called Mengsk crazy."

"So you two agreed on something. I'm amazed."

"Yeah," said Raynor. Then there was a pause. "Yeah, I guess we did."

Arcturus Mengsk was starting to rally troops now to his banner, and when Raynor and Mike arrived on the surface, the assault to rescue the downed battle-cruiser was already under way.

The units that barreled across the flats now included Antigan rebels, Sons of Korhal, and Confederate stragglers that had discarded their loyalties and kept their weapons. Raynor rode at the left flank of a flight of Vulture hover-cycles, while overhead a squadron of A-17 Wraith fighters tore through the sky. Huge Goliaths left great splayed footprints in the soft mud, and they soon overtook a unit of Arclite siege tanks, churning across the bottomlands, their support frames pulled up for movement.

The combined forces met resistance almost immediately. Zerglings and hydralisks spattered on all sides of them, like bugs on a windshield. The air was filled with both the organic cannons (now known to Mike and the rest of human space as mutalisks) and creatures that looked like jellyfish brains with lobster claws; they drifted over the alien forces like stormclouds in the desert.

There was a cluster of marines off to Mike's right, swarming up the sides of what looked like a giant upright zergling, a titanic creature with front claws like huge, hooked sabers. On the horizon, something that looked like a cross between a flying squid and a giant starfish fled from the assault of the Wraith fighters.

They plowed through the Zerg forces, routing some, eliminating others. A group of zerglings erupted from the ground and took out a full unit of marines before the Vultures arrived and laid down a blanket of withering fire.

The Zerg fell back, returned in greater numbers, then fell back again. Mike felt he was fighting the sea. The waves were being beaten back, but he was sure that it was an illusion. The tide was coming in, and it would return in greater force.

In his gut Mike knew that Antiga Prime was damned, as damned as Chau Sara and Mar Sara had been. These things were burrowing through the heart of the world, and either they would be successful or the Protoss would burn them from space.

The Zerg line stiffened for a moment, then broke again, and the humans were through, heading for the uplands where the *Norad II* went down.

With one glance at the starship, Mike could see that the old behemoth would never fly again. Its rear engine pods had been twisted at a forty-five degree angle to the rest of the structure, and the lower landing struts, if they had even been deployed, had been mired totally in the mud. The ship's forward bridge hung precariously over the edge of the mesa, with a view of the devastation beneath it.

Mike and Raynor gunned their engines for an open hatchway and drove their Vultures on board. They sealed the hatch behind them manually, while outside another wave of mutalisks popped up over the horizon.

"Which way?" asked Raynor, pulling off his helmet.

"Come on," said Mike, tearing off toward the bridge. He moved through the tight spaces of the *Norad II* effortlessly, despite his combat armor. He had noticed that Mengsk provided larger hallways on his ship than the Confederacy managed.

It was as if Duke had never left the bridge. The silverbacked gorilla was still hunched over his station in his armored hide. The only change was the number of screens around him that showed nothing but static, and a cascade of fiber-optic cables draped along one bulkhead. He turned to the newcomers and scowled.

"You're about the last folks I expected to show up," he growled.

"Yeah, we love you, too, General," said Mike, pushing his way to the ship's comm unit. He punched in the communication code for Mengsk's base.

"What's all this about?" Duke barked.

"A word from our sponsor," said Mike. "It feels like years since I last said that. Anyone got a cig?"

On the screen, the static-scarred form of Arcturus Mengsk formed. Mengsk, thought Mike, safe in his secret redoubt while the rest of us did the fighting and bleeding.

Mike didn't think it possible, but Duke's scowl deepened. "What's your angle, Mengsk?" he asked.

"Our angle?" Raynor snarled. "I'll give you an *angle*, you slimy Confederate piece of . . ."

"Easy, Jim," said Mike.

"In case you haven't noticed," said Mengsk, "the Confederacy is falling apart, Duke. Its colonies are in open revolt. The Zerg are rampaging unchecked. What would have happened here today if we hadn't shown up?"

"Your point?" Duke kept a stone face.

Mike checked the other screens. Another Wraith

attack had dispersed the mutalisks, but the flying starfish looked to be made of tougher stuff.

"I'm giving you a choice," Mengsk said smoothly. "You can go back to the Confederacy and lose, or you can join us and help save our entire race from being overrun by the Zerg."

"You expect me to answer that?"

"I don't think it's a difficult decision." A small smile appeared beneath Mengsk's gray-spattered mustache.

"I'm a *general*, for God's sake," Duke exploded.

"Oh yeah," said Mike. "Congratulations. Shall we put it on your tombstone?"

"Michael, please," said Mengsk. "Duke, you're a general without an army. I'm offering you a position on my staff, in my cabinet, not just some backwater post where they shelved you before the war."

"I don't know . . ." said Duke, and Mike saw the warrior waver for a moment. Mengsk had him. Poor Duke, he had been hooked. He just didn't know it yet.

"Don't test my patience, Edmund," said Mengsk. Somewhere beyond the bulkheads, something exploded near the ship. Almost as if it had been planned to punctuate Mengsk's comment.

Duke held the moment for a decorous beat, then said, "All right, Mengsk. You've got a deal."

"You've made the right choice . . . *General* Duke," said Mengsk. "Captain Raynor?"

"Yes, sir?" Raynor was scowling now.

"Escort the general's supporters and equipment to

a safe location." As Mengsk spoke, Duke enabled the ship's self-destruct. In twenty minutes they would be klicks away, and the *Norad II* would be a thermonuclear fireball.

"I hope it takes a lot of Zergs with it," said Mike, as the bridge started to clear very, very fast.

Later, Mike was back at Mengsk's communications center. With the explosion of the *Norad II*, there had been a lull in the fighting. Confederate troops, including the neurally resocialized ones, had switched sides easily with official permission, and now the only enemies to deal with were inhuman.

The downside was that there was no shortage of these.

Mike wrapped up a report on the *Norad II* rescue and shot it into the net. He leaned back and ran a hand through his hair. It felt thinner than before.

A pack of cigarettes, slightly crushed, dropped onto the console, followed by a foil container of matches. Raynor said, "One of the crew of the *Norad* says you're even now."

"Excellent," said Mike, drawing out a coffin nail.

"Sending another report to nowhere?"

"I thought Kerrigan was the mind reader. But yeah. Old habits die hard, though I have the fantasy that someone finds these reports years later and appreciates all the sacrifice of men and women against these things. And all the stupidity as well."

Raynor settled down into a chair across from him as Mike lit up. "Unlikely. Like Mengsk says, the victors write the histories. Losing memoirs are deleted like yesterday's data."

Mike took a deep draw and coughed, making a face. "What did they marinate these in, cat urine?"

Raynor raised his hands. "Best I could find, under the circumstances. Story of our lives."

"You betcha," said Mike. "Speaking of the *uber*-Mengsk, how did your talk with Arcturus go?"

"I told him that Duke was a snake." Raynor sighed. "And he said . . ."

"That he was *our* snake, right?"

Raynor shook his head in disbelief. "I believe in Mengsk's cause, that the Confederacy has to go, and he did get me out of stir, but, man. Some of the deals he's making. Some of the things he's asking us to do . . ."

"Don't go following causes," said Mike, taking a painful puff. "They'll just break your heart. When idealism meets reality, it's rarely reality that backs down. I've seen more good government types turn into political hacks than I've seen zerglings. And I've seen a lot of zerglings."

There was a silence between the two men. In the background the muted comm units spoke of mutalisks and Wraiths, of Goliaths and hydralisks, and the starfish things, which they were calling Zerg queens. And death. They spoke incessantly of death.

"I tell you I was married once?" Raynor volunteered.

The chasm of personal interaction yawned wide and deep at Mike's feet. "It hasn't come up," he said calmly, hoping that he was not expected to share back.

"Married. Had a kid. He was 'gifted,' they said."

"I heard the quotation marks around that. Gifted like in ghost material? Psionic powers? Telepathic?"

"Uh-huh. Sent him off to a special school. Government scholarship. A few months later, we got a letter. There had been an 'incident' at the school."

Mike had heard of such letters. They were unfortunately as common as grass when dealing with telepaths. Another of the Confederacy's dirty little secrets, rarely broadcast. "I'm sorry," Mike said, because that was all he could say.

"Yeah. Liddy never recovered. She just sort of wasted away, that winter she went down with the flu. And afterwards, I threw myself into my work. Found out I liked working alone."

"It's an easy trap to fall into, hiding in your work," said Mike, looking at the *transmit* light of his comm link, which meant his report was being sent out into the void.

"Anyway, I wanted you to know," said Raynor. "You may have thought I was being hard on Kerrigan for being a telepath. Maybe I was. But I have my reasons."

"She's got her own problems, you know. Like everybody else, and like no one you've ever met. You might want to cut her a little slack."

"It's kind of hard, when she knows what you're really thinking."

"Kerrigan seems to be a good soldier," said Mike, the image of her as a death-dealing dervish rising unbidden to his mind. "She may be wound a little tight, that's all."

"I think she's dangerous," said Raynor. "Dangerous to the troops around her. Dangerous to Mengsk. And dangerous to herself."

Mike shrugged, unsure how much he could comfortably reveal to the ex-marshal. He settled at last for "She's had a tough life."

"And we've had it easy so far?"

"All the more reason to keep an eye on her. Watch her back. Whether she knows it or not, though she probably will. We all need guardian angels."

The conversation shifted after that to questions of what worlds were in rebellion and what effect Duke's defection would have on other military leaders. Finally Raynor took his leave and abandoned Mike to the soft urgency of the communications room.

Mike looked at the half-empty pack of cigarettes. The taste of the first one was still pungent in his mouth.

"Hell," he said, reaching for the pack and the matches. "I guess, around here, you can learn to tolerate just about *anything*."

CHAPTER 11

CHESS

I played chess with Arcturus Mengsk. I lost regularly, by the way. Someday I'll probably be dragged before some high justice and told that this was a crime against the state, but I will have no defense. Other than losing more times than I won. More often than not, Mengsk would dangle some bait in front of me in a game, and I would snap at it, only to discover too late that I had been distracted from the trap he was setting.

The entire human campaign against the Zerg was similar, consisting of a series of defeats, each one more galling than the last because each time we ignored what was really going on. Our first warning that the Zerg were planetside came usually too late, when the creep appeared at our doorsteps or the Protoss warped in with the thunder-god ships.

We thought we could escape it. Some of us, including Mengsk himself, thought we could control it. But we were all pawns in a greater game.

No, not pawns. Dominos. Each falling in turn, planet

after planet, person after person, until we reached the biggest domino of them all, the one called Tarsonis.

—THE LIBERTY MANIFESTO

"THE COMPARISON HAS BEEN MADE BETWEEN war and chess," said Arcturus Mengsk, forking his knight to threaten both Mike's queen and his bishop.

"You're very good at both," said Mike, moving his queen to take Mengsk's rook.

"Actually, I find the comparison to be false," said the terrorist, moving his knight to take the bishop. "Checkmate, by the way."

Mike blinked at the board. Mengsk's strategy was obvious now, in the same way that it had been totally opaque mere seconds before. The reporter mentally kicked himself and reached for his brandy snifter. In the background, the lost tunes of ancient Miller and Goodman warbled out of the comm unit. The ashtray to one side of the board was filled with butts, all of them Mike's. They smelled faintly of cat urine.

They were on board the *Hyperion*, resting in a hidden hanger on Antiga Prime. Duke was off reorganizing the rebel troops into something that was more Confederate in nature. Raynor was off trying to keep Duke from making a complete mess of things. Mike had no idea where Kerrigan was, but that was normal for Kerrigan.

"Chess is not like war?" Mike asked.

"Once, perhaps, it was," said Mengsk. "On Old

Earth, back in the mists of time. Two equal opponents, with equal forces, on a level playing field."

"And that's not the case. Not anymore."

"Hardly," said the terrorist, warming to his own discussion. "First, the opponents are hardly ever truly even. The Confederacy of Man had Apocalypse-class missiles and my homeworld did not; the Confederacy played that card until Korhal IV was a blackened glass sphere hanging in space. Hardly even. Similarly, our little rebellion seemed at first to be undermanned and underfunded, but with each new revolt the Confederacy loses more of its will to fight. It is ancient and rotten, and all it needs is a good push to cave it in. You don't see that in chess.

"Second," Mengsk continued, "is the idea of equal forces. I mentioned the missiles, so effective in my father's time, yet mere pinpricks in the light of the forces being wielded today. Forces continue to evolve—nukes, telepaths, now Zerg being raised by the Confederacy."

"War is supposed to increase development," said Mike.

"Yes, but most people use the guns and armor analogy: one side gets a better gun, the other side gets better armor, which inspires a still better gun, and so on. The truth is that a better gun inspires a chemical counterweapon, which then inspires a telepathic strike, which then brings about an artificial intelligence guiding the weapon. The pressure of war does bring about growth, but it is never the neat, linear growth that you learn about in the classroom."

"Or read about in the papers."

Mengsk smiled. "Third is the idea of a level playing field. The chessboard is limited to an eight-by-eight grid. There is nothing beyond this little universe. No ninth rank. No green pieces that suddenly sweep onto the board to attack both black and white. No pawns that suddenly become bishops."

"A pawn can become a queen," Mike noted.

"But only by advancing through all the spaces of its row, under fire the entire time. It doesn't suddenly blossom into a queen by its own volition. No, chess is nothing like war, which is one of the reasons I play it. It's so much simpler than real life."

Not for the first or last time, Mike thought about Mengsk's almost supernatural ability to warp reality around himself. "You think that the Confederacy is going to be able to come up with a weapon against these latest attacks? Against the Protoss and the Zerg?"

"Unlikely, though they are pulling out all the stops. Doing what they do best right now: propaganda and silencing those who speak out. Those are their best weapons, and they have never hesitated to use them before. But they're just throwing spitwads at a bull elephant that's bearing down on them. Hang on, I've got something here I wanted to show you." Mengsk pressed numerous buttons on a remote control. He stared at it, as if trying to remember a secret code.

"I thought you once said that the Confederacy was

breeding the Zerg. Doesn't that make the Zerg their weapons?" Mike asked.

"Originally I thought so as well." Mengsk pressed a few more buttons, then paused. "And though I may be incorrect in the assumption, as far as *our* propaganda is concerned, that's our story, and we're sticking with it. Nothing undermines faith in the government faster than realizing that they've been developing deadly alien menaces in their spare time."

"But the truth really is?" Mike prompted.

"The truth is as malleable as ever." Mengsk grinned. "Yes, the Confederacy has been studying the Zerg for years, and the ones in the Sara system were deliberately brought there by Confederate agents. Yes, they were a big weapons test. But no, they didn't create the Zerg. No, they had a much worse plan in mind. It was on those disks that you and Raynor brought back from the Jacobs Installation. Here we go. You'll appreciate this."

He hit a button, and the screen sprang to scratchy life. When the distortion had cleared, Mike could see a string of low buttes and mesas beneath an orange-brown sky. The scene could have been anywhere on Antiga Prime. The familiar UNN logo perched along one side, and multiplanetary stock prices crawled across the bottom of the screen.

Then a frighteningly familiar voice spoke over the panorama. "This is Michael Liberty, reporting from Antiga Prime."

Mike blinked. That was his voice, part of his last

transmission out. But he had never sent this particular footage. Had they pulled it from a file somewhere?

The camera continued to pan, then settled on the speaker. He was dressed in a neat duster (much neater than the one that currently hung in Mike's locker), his blond hair pulled back to cover a bald spot, his features hard-chiseled and experienced, his eyes deep and soulful.

It was Michael Liberty, but not Mike. This Michael Liberty looked almost like an idealized version of Mike himself.

The figure on the screen continued, "This reporter has just escaped captivity at the hands of the infamous terrorist Arcturus Mengsk. I was captured on Mar Sara by the rebels shortly before the reptilian Protoss destroyed the planet, and have only made it to safety now."

"That's not me," said Mike.

"I know," said Mengsk. "And the Protoss aren't reptiles, as far as we know. But keep watching."

"During my captivity I learned that Mengsk and the Sons of Korhal are in control of powerful mind-control drugs, which they have been using freely on the populace," continued the flat-screen Mike Liberty. "Hundreds have died as a result of indiscriminate spraying, which can only be described as chemical attacks against innocent citizens. Others have been warped into strange mutagenic shapes as a result of side effects of these drugs."

Mengsk made a rude noise, but the figure on the

screen continued, "Mengsk sent a saboteur aboard the *Norad II* and exposed the crew to a virulent toxin. The result was the recent crash of that ship. Agents of the Sons of Korhal captured those affected by the mind-control drugs, and left the rest to die at the hands of their Zerg allies."

"Zerg allies? Who's writing that crap?" Mike snapped at the screen.

"It *is* much of muchness," Mengsk said calmly. "Laying it on a bit thick and all."

"I believe that General Edmund Duke, scion of the Duke Family of Tarsonis, has fallen prey to these mind-control devices, and now has been reduced to a mentally reprogrammed zombie in the service of the terrorists. In this way Mengsk and his inhuman allies hope to confuse the brave warriors of the Confederacy and cause them to lose faith in their leaders."

"Brave warriors of the . . . I used that line in a filler piece I did on the *Norad II!*" said Mike. "And the bit about 'virulent toxins.' That rings another bell."

"Groundwater pollution outside a middle school," said Mengsk. "One of your better early pieces, if I remember right."

"Only by eternal vigilance can we root out such terrorists as Mengsk and his mind-controlled minions," said the figure on the screen. "As I speak a massive Confederate blockade is surrounding Antiga Prime, and the terrorist should be destroyed within a few days. This is Michael Daniel Liberty for UNN."

Mengsk hit another button. Michael Daniel Liberty froze into silence on the screen.

"Did you see that!?" Mike shouted, jumping up from his seat. "That wasn't me!"

"I hope not," Mengsk said with a calm grin. "You seem like such a rational and truthful reporter, most of the time."

"What did they do?"

"You've never been edited before?" Mengsk raised an eyebrow.

"Of course!" Mike snapped, then added quickly, "I mean for time, or if the facts couldn't be confirmed, or the legal department had a problem, or a sponsor raised a stink. I mean, I've had things cut before, and sometimes they've slid in images that took the tone of the story in a different direction. But this is a . . . a . . ."

"Lie?"

"Fabrication," Mike said, frowning.

"Indeed. Clipped together from bits of previous reporting, using another actor as a stand-in, a shuffling of pixels. Mind you, it's easy enough on a flat screen—damned impossible with a true hologram. That's why I prefer the latter, you know. This is just enough to fool someone just catching the news, to remind them that you're alive and well and fighting the good fight for UNN and the Confederacy."

"But my reports . . ." Mike sputtered.

"Grist that they took apart and reassembled as they saw fit."

Mike slouched back into his chair. "I'm going to *kill* Anderson."

"Your Anderson may already be dead, I'm afraid," said the terrorist. "If he's as devoted a reporter as you."

Mike snorted.

"Or," Mengsk reconsidered, "he may be acquiescing to the current power structure, though he knows it's a horrible idea. Maybe that's why the 'toxic poisons' line is in there—a bit of internal sabotage, a desperate cry for help. I mean, it doesn't make a whole lot of sense: Why would mind-control drugs be poisons? Of course, it did let them lift an entire sentence verbatim."

"Yeah, that's a shortcut Handy Anderson would take."

"I just wanted you to know that your own network has turned its back on you. I didn't want you to find out at a bad time. Like on the battlefield, for example." Mengsk refilled Mike's snifter.

"But why this?"

"Propaganda is a weapon that the Confederacy wields best, and wields heaviest. It is their hammer. And when all you have is a hammer, then everything looks like a nail."

"You'd think they'd have better weapons than a reporter to throw at you," Mike muttered. He shook his head at the screen. "What happened to all their Zerg research, the material we got out of that installation?"

"Ah." Mengsk hit another series of buttons. "The

Jacobs disk. I'm glad you remembered that—it shows that my mind-control drugs have not had a complete effect on you. Don't look at me that way, it was meant as a joke."

"I'm a little sensitive about that right now. It'll pass."

"I expected weapons data—something to keep them ahead of the technological curve. Instead I found something much more interesting. Here we go. You know about ghosts, of course."

Mike thought of Kerrigan, the merciless fighter who felt the death of each of her victims. "Telepathic warriors. A specialty of the Confederates, and an example of your technological curve."

"An interesting example, if I may digress. The original inhabitants of the colony ships were Earth people, but the long voyage apparently put a twist in their genetic code, enough to bring out more psionic abilities than were common in the original Terran populace. An interesting happenstance."

"I think we've both gotten to the point where we don't believe in happenstance." Mike took a pull on his brandy.

Mengsk gave a good-natured shrug. "By design or accident, the humans of what would become the Confederacy tended toward psychic abilities. Again, through design or accident, we found this out and created the ghosts—superior assassins with mind-reading powers. It's a horrible process—only a few children make it out of the process in any usable state.

And, until recently, the Confederate's control over them seemed unbreakable."

"Lieutenant Sarah Kerrigan. How did you break their control over her?"

"That's a case where one side gets better armor, and the other side gets a bigger gun," Mengsk said with a smile. "Suffice it to say that the control over her was broken, and broken in such a way that she was left amazingly intact and generally useful."

"And grateful."

"And grateful," Mengsk admitted. "And she has appeared often enough that the Confederates are in a tizzy about it."

"Which suits you just fine," said Mike. "But you were busy digressing?"

"Yes. Now we get to the Jacobs disk. It turns out that our pestilent friends the Zerg are attuned to psychic emanations. Apparently the wavelengths that the ghosts function on are similar to those that the higher-level Zerg use to control the lesser ones. So they can zero in on them at close range."

"How close?" Mike asked, thinking suddenly of Kerrigan's activities in the Sara and Antiga systems.

"For a normal telepath, very, very close. Tens of yards at best. By that time a hydralisk can smell them anyway. But that's part of the technology the Confederates have used in their tower defenses and other anti-ghost detectors."

"Guns and armor. Can the ghosts read Zerg minds like they do humans'?"

"It's much more painful. And yes, the Confederates tried. They came away with the idea that the Zerg are an ultimate evolutionary success stories: everything is either genetic material for their creations or meat to be fed to their children. They operate off a hierarchy of hive minds, each greater than the ones below it, growing up to near-planetary consciousnesses."

"Sounds appealing." Mike took another long sip of his brandy. It burned the back of his throat and reminded him he was human.

"Nasty. The Protoss are as bad," said Mengsk. "Mind you, this is all from the Zerg viewpoint that's recorded on the disks, but the Protoss are the ultimate genetic purists. They see themselves as the judges of the universe, eradicating any life that gets out of hand and does not meet their standard of perfection."

"Genetic Survivors versus Genetic Xenophobes. A match made in hell."

"Very much so. So the Confederates discover the Zerg and discover the telepathic attraction. They want more Zerg available."

"More? Why in the name of God would they want more?"

"The nonlinear nature of war, son. They were looking for a weapon with all the advantages of nukes and none of the downside, like radiation or bad press. The Zergs were perfect—they were ugly-buggy aliens that the Confederates could unleash on anyone, and then come in afterwards and eliminate. A pocket plague of monsters."

"You said you thought they were breeding them."

"And I was wrong about that," Mengsk said smoothly, "Breeding them is much more complex than just capturing a bunch of zerglings and putting them in the same cage. So they needed to lure more into their traps, and that's where the telepaths came in."

"But the telepaths have limited range."

"Yes," Mengsk agreed. "So they worked on improving that range. What you pulled out of the Jacobs Installation was the plans for a Transplanar Psionic Waveform Emitter. Nice name, and fairly self-descriptive. With it they could boost the power of a telepath and make it an interplanetary beacon for the Zerg, drawing them in like moths to a lantern."

Mike was silent for a moment, then said, "The Sara system."

"Exactly. That's what I mean when I say they were using those planets as a testing ground for their weapons. They brought the Zerg to Sara, and the Protoss came after them. But they brought more than just a couple zerglings—they brought the whole Zerg ecosystem and power structure into play, which they *didn't* expect. And now the Zerg are moving from system to system at will, directed by their own intelligence, intent on either transforming humanity or consuming it."

"So you know how to defeat them?" Mike asked.

"Other than blasting each and every one of them into bits and burning their nests, no." Mengsk leaned forward. "But I do know how to send them in the directions I want them to go."

"How does that help?" Mike shook his head. Had the brandy made him suddenly stupid?

Mengsk leaned back. "There was one piece of truth in that news report your doppelgänger delivered. There is a serious blockade forming around Antiga. The Confederates are hoping to keep us penned up until either the Zerg or the Protoss destroy us."

"And we're just sitting here?"

"No. I'm already doing something. We built an emitter, based on the plans you liberated. We're going to take it into the heart of Confederate territory and set it off. Every Zerg from as far away as ten light-years is going to come here. They're going to fall among the blockaders like falcons on doves. The crash of the *Norad II* will be a simple fender bender in comparison."

"But the emitter will only amplify. You need a telepath to . . ." The final circuit closed in Mike's brain. "Kerrigan. You're going to use Kerrigan to bring in the Zerg."

"Very good."

"You can't do that!" Mike objected. "You want her to break into a Confederate camp? They'll have detectors. She'll never make it!"

"I have a high degree of confidence in the lieutenant."

"You can't do that!" Mike repeated.

"You have your tense wrong. I gave the orders for the operation before we sat down for our first game. The good lieutenant should be picking up the emitter in the shops below right about now. If you hurry, you can catch up with her."

Mike cursed and launched himself from his seat.

"And wish her luck from me!" Mengsk shouted at Mike's back as the reporter bolted out of the terrorist leader's quarters. Then Mengsk leaned back, lifted his own brandy snifter, and offered a silent toast to the frozen figure of the false Michael Liberty on the screen.

CHAPTER 12

BELLY OF THE BEAST

Aliens were pressing in on human space, and the humans reacted by turning on one another. I can only imagine what the Zerg and the Protoss thought as they landed on planets that consisted of nothing but rebels and Confederates whaling the tar out of each other. They probably thought it was the normal behavior pattern for our race. And I suppose they would be right.

Mengsk's successes, spread in part by bootleg copies of my own reports, sparked dozens of brushfire wars. Every crank with a gripe took up arms against the ancient Confederate regime. The Confederacy in turn reacted as it always had to armed dissent—with harsher and harsher oppression that in turn spawned other revolts.

And through it all, the Zerg were infiltrating more planets, and the Protoss were turning them to dead lumps. The humans didn't have so many worlds that they could afford to lose them at this clip. If the two sides had been thinking, they would have joined forces to fight the true menace.

I think everybody was so busy planning and fighting that no one really had time to think.

—THE LIBERTY MANIFESTO

"KERRIGAN!" MIKE SHOUTED IN THE LANDING Bay. The lieutenant was just putting on her helmet. He had no time for armor, but he did grab his duster.

"Liberty," she said grimly. Mike saw a large device mounted to the side of her Vulture bike. "I'm just heading out."

"Ride shotgun?"

"Look, normally I'd . . ." she began, then looked at Mike with her deep jade-green eyes. The hairs on the back of Mike's neck stood up, and he knew that she knew.

Her too-wide lips twitched for a moment. Then she shook her head and said, "It's your funeral. I'll need someone to lug the gear anyway. Come on."

The pair roared out of the hangar, making for the rendezvous point.

Antiga Prime had suffered under the relentless assault. The sky was darker now from the smoke of continuous pyres, and the great bloated figure of the world's gas giant primary hung like a sorrowful god behind a shroud of mourning. In the distance there was the thunder of Arclite artillery, though who was firing, and who they were firing at, was unknown.

They passed abandoned bunkers, cracked open like eggshells, surrounded by the partially buried detritus of war: broken weapons and shattered men. The thunder grew louder, and Liberty realized they were heading into the heart of the storm.

"We've got siege tanks and Goliaths," Kerrigan said over the comm link, "trying to punch a hole in their lines. We slip through and into Confederate territory. Regret coming now?"

"Maybe a little." Mike knew that the ghost knew his answer even before he spoke.

"So Mengsk gave you the whole song and dance," she continued. Mike frowned, concerned that the telepath was rummaging through his thoughts so easily. "Got you to come along."

"Check my mental replay again, Lieutenant," said Mike. "Mengsk never asked me to go."

"He didn't have to. He knows the buttons to press on people. Probably he felt that if he ordered you to come help, you'd probably just dump him then and there."

"He's probably right."

"He usually is. That's why it's probably a good idea you're along."

Up ahead, a pile of boulders vaporized in a massive explosion. Kerrigan brought the cycle up short.

"That shouldn't happen," she said. "Our siege tanks know we're coming this way. Did Duke screw up his artillery spotting on purpose, or . . ."

Mike heard the whistling of another set of incoming rounds. "It's their tanks!" he shouted. "They've broken through *our* lines!"

Kerrigan gunned the engine the moment he said it,

tearing the Vulture at a sharp angle to its original course of travel. The road ahead vanished in a crescendo of flying earth and rock as another round tracked closer. The shattered earth was too much for the limited grav units, and the entire bike shook.

"It's a bit—" Mike began.

"Sorry for the rough ride," Kerrigan snapped over the comm link. "Just hang on!"

Next time let me finish my sentence, thought Mike, and felt Kerrigan shrug on the bike.

The Confederates must have had a spotter. The missile fire tracked them mercilessly, staying about a hundred yards behind them. Kerrigan took them into a ravine that had long since lost anything that looked like water.

"Let's see them follow in here," she said.

Mike heard the high-pitched whine of metal slicing through air, "Wraiths!" he yelled into the comm link.

The fighter spacecraft came in low and hard, blasting both sides of the ravine with their 25-millimeter burst-lasers. The scrub was incinerated at a touch, and the fighters pulled up, unable to see their prey through the smoke they had generated.

"They're herding us," Kerrigan's voice crackled over the comm link. "But to where?"

The ground beneath the hover-cycle suddenly changed in texture, from red clays and brownish slates to a mottled clumping of gray-black moss.

"Creep!" said Mike, as soon as he had recognized it. "They're herding us into Zerg territory!"

Kerrigan cursed and threw on the brakes, but the creep beneath the grav-fields provided no traction for the bike's transducer coils. The thin bike started to fishtail, then skewed horribly to one side, plowing up a thick crust of the creep like foam on a wave.

Mike shouted, and Kerrigan yelled something. The reporter clutched the container of the psi emitter, half hoping that it would provide some protection. He was sure that if anyone could get them through this, it would be the ghost lieutenant.

Then the ground opened up beneath them, and they both tumbled into the darkness.

Sometime later, Mike heard Kerrigan's voice, as if from a distance, "Liberty?"

"Urg," was the best Mike could reply. *Hell, she can read my mind, let her read this.*

"Is the psi emitter all right?" she asked.

"Oh yeah. I cushioned its fall with my body."

He opened his eyes and discovered he was lying in soft, recently churned earth. That must have been what broke their fall as they pitched down the rabbit hole.

He looked up. There was a jagged hole in the ceiling, probably where they tore through the creep matting. Already the thick webbing was reknitting across the opening.

Mike spat out some blood. He had bitten the inside of his mouth in the fall. The rest of his body seemed battered but generally unharmed. His duster was caked with soft earth. He would feel the bruises tomorrow.

If I'm lucky, he thought.

"If we're both lucky," said Kerrigan. She was already on her feet, sweeping the area with a wrist-mounted light. She had slung her canister rifle over her shoulder.

Mike stood up, and found himself wobbling but unhurt. "Y'all right?" he managed.

"Not bad," said the ghost. "I landed on my pride, which is, I'm afraid, a lost cause. Had to shoot it, put it out of its misery. We're patsies. Fools. Mooks. Rubes."

"No one expected the Confederates—" Mike began.

"To use the terrain and situation to their advantage? Exactly. Which is why we're patsies. They came out to meet our attack, and then flushed us into the one place we don't want to be."

"You know, this would be easier if you—"

"Let you finish your sentences. Sorry. Nervous habit right now. You're practically broadcasting your fear, and that's irritating *me.*"

Like anybody wouldn't be afraid in this situation, Mike thought, walking over to the remains of the Vulture bike.

"The bike is shot," Kerrigan said, without looking, and of course she was right. The frame was bent in three places, so that the long, lean vehicle had been turned into a twisted corkscrew. Something important had been punctured and was leaking into the ground.

The bike, in spite of all its metal and shaped ceramic, had taken the fall worse than he had.

"This way," said Kerrigan, pointing sharply one way along the corridor.

"Any clue why?"

"No, but something large and foul-thinking is in the other direction. You get to carry the emitter."

Mike hoisted the emitter in its container and followed. He thought about the lieutenant's mood. After a few minutes Kerrigan said, "It's a feedback loop."

"Stop *doing* that."

"But it is. Your fear is sent to me, and I'm in turn taking it out on you. Which increases *your* anger." She paused for a moment. "Something's real strange here. Wrong. I can handle this kind of thing normally. Most of the time."

Mike thought of the Zerg's supposed connection with telepaths, then wished he hadn't.

Kerrigan's too-wide lips twisted in a grim smile. "Yeah, I know. Raynor already gave me grief about it at the briefing with Arcturus, thank you very much. It does explain the Confederacy's interest in telepaths. And also there have been a lot of MIAs among the Confederate telepaths. Even outside the ghost units, I hear things."

"Think the Zerg are collecting their own telepath subjects?" Mike asked, then realized that Kerrigan had let him finish his sentence.

"Uh-huh. Hang on, something's up ahead." She

pulled out her side arm and edged forward, her other hand, the one with the wristlight, pointing ahead.

The something was hanging across the passageway like a great spider. Her light flashed against it, and it shrank away from the beam. It was a great eye, human in appearance, its pupil contracting under the harshness of the wristlight's beam.

Mike felt a wave of revulsion and nausea sweep over him. Apparently Kerrigan felt it as well, and her emotions were compounded through Mike's mind. She let out a loud curse and fired a short burst into the twitching orb.

The eye-thing let out a screech that sounded like glass and blew apart, the muscular strands of its web peeling back toward the wall like broken rubber bands.

"What was—?" Mike began.

"Observer? Sentry?" Kerrigan guessed, and for the first time Mike caught a bit of fear in the unshakable Sarah Kerrigan's voice. Feedback loop, he reminded himself. He willed himself to calm down. Otherwise they would get themselves killed.

"What does it feel like?" he asked, as they edged past the shredded meat of the eye-thing. Mike noticed that there was creep along the floors and walls of the passage.

"What?" said Kerrigan, distracted by the ichor.

"You said it felt strange down here. Strange?"

Kerrigan was silent for a moment, and Mike felt she was trying to regain her emotional strength. "It's tough to describe to a hard-shell, sorry, a nontelepath. It's like you're in a hotel hallway and there's a party in one of the rooms. As you pass it, you hear that there's a party, but it's not yours. You don't make out anything distinct, but there's a babble of voices. That's what it feels like."

"Maybe psionic power on a different channel?" Mike suggested.

"Maybe, but it's larger. Like standing on a street outside a theater where there's a concert. You hear something organized, but all you make out is blather. It's maddening." She paused for a moment. "Oh my God. Mike, come here."

The passage opened out to the right, into a larger cavern, before continuing upward. Mike could feel fresher air on his face from the passage across the way. They must be near the surface.

The larger cavern was filled with creep. Vague pouches hung from the walls, and things that might have been organs dotted the grayish fungus. Along the wall was a scattering of centipede-like creatures moving among a field of toadstools.

"Maggots," said Mike. "I saw them at Anthem Base, on Mar Sara." He shot an image of the bar there to Kerrigan, and noticed her shudder. "Is this a garbage dump for the Zerg? What are they eating?"

"They're not eating. They're nursemaids. They're tending the eggs."

What Mike had first thought of as toadstools were really eggs, green with reddish speckles, that sat on stands of piled creep. The eggs pulsed with their own heartbeats. As Mike watched, the skeletal face of a hydralisk appeared beneath the murky surface of the nearest egg, like a drowned creature in a tidal pool. The egg quivered a little, as if the beast within knew of their presence.

The maggots were busy building up piles of the creep. Then one climbed the pile, curled in on itself, and wove a thick spider-silk cocoon around itself. The cocoon hardened, and the maggot became an egg.

"Crap," said Mike, suddenly realizing what the maggots were.

"Larvae. They're the basic building units of the Zerg. Larvae to eggs to monsters. That's why the Confederates never got anywhere breeding the suckers, despite what Mengsk said. The zerglings and hydralisks *can't* breed— they all come from the same genetic stock, served up to order from some higher power."

Mike nodded, and the hydralisk face in the egg turned toward him. The egg started to vibrate violently as the beast within tried to force itself out.

"Head toward the fresh air," said Kerrigan, unslinging her canister rifle. "I'll be along in a moment."

Grunting under the load of the emitter, Mike continued up the corridor. When he heard the whirring noise of the canister rifle's feed and the sliding ratchet of its pump action, he started running. Behind him now was the hammering chatter of the rifle's sharp-tipped bullets strafing the egg chamber. Then there was silence.

The air grew fresher, and he saw natural light up ahead. Mike's legs felt like lead weights, but he forced them forward. Ten more yards, then five, then two. Then up to the surface, into the early evening air, and . . .

Face-to-face with his reflection in the mirrored surface of a Confederate marine's combat visor. Despite himself, Mike yelped and almost fell backward. A sentry from the Confederate forces was posted at the entrance.

The sentry lumbered a step toward the reporter, and Mike realized that something was wrong with the man. His knees were bent oddly, and his arms seemed to belong to separate entities. One hand raised a gauss rifle uncertainly, while the other touched something at the base of its armor.

The mirrored visor slid back to reveal a face from hell. Half of it had been eaten away to the yellow-stained skull, which oozed a thick grayish creep from a useless eyehole. The other half, the greenish shade of rot, was studded with rock-like extrusions that broke the skin like short daggers.

It was a sentry, but not for the Confederates. It had once been human, but not now. It had once been sane, but not now. Now it only lived to protect the nest. It brought up its gauss rifle and let out a cry as if coins were caught in its throat. The creature's good eye seemed to weep blood.

Mike heard the whine of the canister rifle behind him and threw himself to the ground, twisting to cushion the emitter as he toppled. An instant later the air where he had been was filled with live rounds. A few of the rounds shredded the edge of his coat.

The transformed Confederate sentry was transfixed by the rifle fire, but only for a moment. Then its gauss rifle slowly spilled from its hand and it fell backward, its armor in tatters. What lay beneath the armor was no longer human, but it reacted to the canister shot in the same fashion.

Kerrigan ran up and tugged hard on Mike's collar. "Are you okay?"

Spots danced in front of Mike's eyes, but he refused to succumb to the bitter bile rising in his throat. "What *was* that?"

"The Zerg are master biologists. That's probably what they want to do with humanity. Turn it into another experiment. Another servant race."

Mike took a deep breath, looking at the lacerated, rotting meat, and said, "It doesn't look like a successful experiment."

Kerrigan gave an exhausted shrug. "Maybe if they had better material to work with. You volunteering? I'm sure they need a reporter." She managed a tight, chiding grin, and despite himself, Mike let out a chuckle.

Breaking the feedback loop, he thought. Foxhole jokes. Gallows humor in the face of the obscenity of war.

If Kerrigan read those thoughts, she did not let on. "Feel like running for a while?" she asked.

"How far?"

"As far as we can."

"You start, I'll follow," said Mike, hoisting the emitter in front of him.

They were lucky. They were on the edge of the creep. Yet even from their vantage point Mike could see a line of towers in the direction opposite their line of travel. They looked like great, misshapen flowers from some giant's garden, and the cannon-like mutalisks danced among them. There were other flying monsters as well, including the starfish squids, the lobster-jellyfishes, and the great flying crabs.

"They're winning," said Mike. "The Zerg. They're getting more powerful every damned planet they take over."

"Try not to think about it." Kerrigan touched her wrist. "I just sent out a short pulse-message. If Arcturus is listening, at least he'll know we're still alive."

Travel was easy now, for even as the sun set there was strong reflected light from the gas giant above. To their left there were more flashes along the horizon, and the sound of distant thunder.

"You say you heard about other ghosts going MIA. You hear from them?" Mike asked.

Kerrigan's lips made a firm line, and she shook her head. "Most telepaths avoid one another. I don't even talk to the ones in Duke's command. It's bad enough being around the continual chatter of normal people. Being with another telepath is a hundred times worse. People can't control their thoughts, at least not very well. Ghosts read other ghosts very well, and form their own feedback loops. Most need psionic dampers to keep them sane. That's like the neural resocialization, but much, much worse."

"But you don't have any psionic dampers."

"I still have some, but most of them are gone. Arcturus . . ." She paused for a moment, then said, "You don't like him, you know."

"Never would have guessed. But you think the world of him."

"He . . ." She paused again. "He broke me out, I guess that's the best way to put it. He rescued me, freed me, broke me of the dampers and the guards and the horror. I owe him my life. More important, I owe him my soul."

As if in response to her comment, the comm link beeped. Mike scanned the horizon for movement. Nothing. Kerrigan popped open a small screen, and Mike could envision Mengsk's smiling face there.

"Good to know you're alive," said the rebel leader. "Your position puts you a klick south of where you need to be. No bogeys between you and the Confederate camp. We're drawing off their reserves."

"We were delayed," said Kerrigan. "The Zerg. There are a lot of them already here."

"And there will be more when you set off our little surprise. They'll keep our Confederate friends busy while we escape."

A frown crossed Kerrigan's features. "They'll be wiped

out, Arcturus." Static crossed the line. "Arcturus? Do you read? The Zerg don't take prisoners."

"Kerrigan!" said Mengsk, and Mike could imagine the stern-father look on the terrorist's face. "We didn't invent the emitters, but if we don't use them, we will all die, blockaded by the Confederates. And if we die, all hope of humanity dies with us."

"Yes, sir."

"Remember how much I trust you. And say hello to Mr. Liberty for me, eh?"

Kerrigan closed the screen and turned north. Mike picked up the emitter and followed.

Mike was silent for a while, then said, "I think they're afraid."

"Who? The people in charge of the ghosts?"

"Yeah. They don't want you to be able to communicate your experiences to other telepaths. Conspire against them. That's why the psionic dampers and the training."

Kerrigan shrugged. "That's likely. I think it's also to keep their investments in one piece. The casualty rate is incredibly high among the ghosts."

"I thought you'd be lionized, after all that investment. Like Wraith pilots or destroyer captains."

Kerrigan let out a horrible laugh. "Lionized? God, even the child molesters they put in the marines get better treatment than we do. The criminals in the marines are just medicated and indoctrinated to follow their leaders. We're given the living nightmare of pushing against our restraints constantly, knowing that if we break them, we'll spin out into insanity because we can't keep others' minds out of our own."

"Easy, Lieutenant. I didn't mean—"

"Of course you didn't mean anything," Kerrigan said hotly. "That's what drives us crazy. Your words mean one thing, but your mind's broadcasting something completely different. Raynor's all gung-ho, but I can feel his unease, his disgust. And I know he's watching, even when my back's turned. It's knowing what's on the tip of everyone's mind without being able to respond."

"I'm sorry."

"I know," said Kerrigan, softening a little. "That's one of the things I *do* like about you, Michael Liberty. You're all surface. Don't take that the wrong way. You think of something, and you say it. Your only defense is when you're asking questions, playing the hard-nosed reporter. It makes you easier to tolerate than most humans."

She paused for a moment as they crested a hill. In the distance rose the ruined towers of the Confederates' outer perimeter. There was no fire from the towers; Mengsk's troops had drawn them off.

"You know what the final exam is to get into ghost training?" she asked suddenly. Mike shook his head, knowing better than to interrupt.

"They have a guard with a gun," she said, and her eyes seemed to mist over. She herself was elsewhere. "The guard takes the gun and presses it against your forehead, or the forehead of someone you care about.

You have to kill the guard before he pulls the trigger."
Her eyes refocused, and she looked at Mike hard. "I
was twelve at the time."

Mike blanched, and despite himself, thought of
Raynor's son. The "gifted" child who had experienced
an "incident."

Kerrigan reacted as if Mike had slapped her. She
sank to one knee and gripped her forehead with her
hand. After a while she said, "Christ."

Mike said quickly, "I'm sorry, I didn't mean to tell
you, it just slipped out."

"Christ," she repeated. "I should have guessed. I
just didn't know."

Mike shook his head. "You're a telepath. How can
you not know?"

Kerrigan looked up, and there were tears at the
corners of her eyes. "Telepaths don't dig down into
your thoughts, at least if they want to stay sane. We
hear all the surface chatter, all the stuff that's on the
top. What you're thinking about. Errant thoughts.
Whether that woman has a nice set of legs. All the
stupid crap. Not the stuff they keep buried. Not the
important crap." She was silent for a moment, then
asked, "He say when it happened?"

Mike shook his head and turned away, partly to
keep an eye out for Confederate patrols, partly to give
the lieutenant a chance to pull herself together.

She probably knew that, but when Mike turned back
she was on her feet and her eyes were dry. "Let's plant
this thing. Base of one of those towers should do it."

They reached the shell of the gun emplacement without difficulty, and Mike surrendered the burden he had been lugging for the past few kilometers. With deft, practiced hands, Kerrigan began setting up the psi emitter that she had never handled before. Mike realized that she must have gotten the instructions in a burst of telepathy when she picked up the device.

It was a lash-up, and it took a few minutes for the lieutenant to uncoil all the packing material and check all the leads. Then she pulled out what looked like a starfish-shaped headset and placed in on her head. A crown of delicate copper filigree was lost among her red tresses.

"The transplanar psionic waveform emitter," explained Kerrigan, "is like the sound box of a violin. It will capture, amplify, and then propagate the psychic beacon that is fed into it. That's why we're here—it needs a ghost to activate it."

She flipped a few switches, pressed a toggle, and then took off the headset. Her face looked strained. "Okay. Let's go."

"That's it?"

"You wanted an airhorn and bright light? A chime from above? Or a big clock with a countdown? Sorry." Kerrigan's face was ashen now, and Mike suddenly realized that, even though he couldn't feel it, Kerrigan could, and it was getting "louder" all the time.

"Right," Kerrigan said. "Let's go."

Mike and Kerrigan headed along the line of abandoned tower emplacements, each one a shattered monument to the battle of Antiga Prime. She had to pause, wincing from the unheard noise. It was as if she could hear nails on a chalkboard, a grating sound that Mike was deaf to.

They made it to the fourth tower, where the pain seemed to ease. By the sixth tower she was almost normal again. She popped open the small screen on her wrist. "Psi emitter in place," she said.

Mengsk's unseen face said, "Excellent, Sarah, I knew you could do it. We've got to get you out before every Zerg on Antiga gets there. Dropship en route."

"I know," Kerrigan said, breathing hard. Her lips formed a thin line, then she said, "Promise me . . . Promise me we'll never do anything like this again."

"Sarah." Mike could imagine Mengsk shaking his head over the line. "We will do whatever it takes to save humanity. Our responsibility is too great to do any less."

And he was gone again, the great wise leader on the far side of the electronic channel, directing the war from the safety of his brandy and chess games.

"Why do you trust him?" Mike asked. The thought had crossed his mind and he said it. "Why do you follow him?"

Sarah managed a weary smile. "He saved my soul."

"And you've been killing for him ever since. Don't the scales ever balance? Aren't you due your own freedom?"

"It's . . . complex. Mengsk is a lot like you. Okay,

I'm sorry, he's actually the complete opposite. You're all surface, like a sheet of newsprint. He's all depth. He tells you what he thinks, and he's so convinced of it, down to the core of his being, that the effect is very much the same. He inspires me to believe."

"He's a politician. If you look deep enough, you'll find that out. There's a bottom to that swamp of his soul."

"And will that change anything? Do I want to look?"

"Sometimes looking isn't a bad thing. If you looked a little harder, then maybe Raynor wouldn't seem like such a jackass."

Kerrigan opened her mouth to say something, then stopped and nodded. "Yeah, you're probably right. At least with Raynor. I guess I owe that much to the jackass."

"Our responsibility is too great to do any less," quoted Mike.

Kerrigan let out a laugh, a short giggle. It was unexpected and unplanned and very human.

Mike let out a long breath and wondered which would arrive first, the Zerg from the nearby colony or Mengsk's promised dropship.

CHAPTER 13

SOUL-SEARCHING

Through the lens of history, war seems to function with a frightening punctuality, like a murderous music box. Battles are no more than clockwork mechanisms of death, a drama of destruction with each act flowing naturally into the next, until one side or the other is vanquished. In retrospect, the fall of the Confederacy seems like a logical slide that, once begun, leaves no question as to its conclusion.

For those of us trapped in the middle of the war, there was nothing but raw panic broken by periods of total exhaustion. No one, not even those who supposedly did the planning, had any clear idea of the forces we were dealing with, until it was too late to change.

Clockwork? Perhaps. But I prefer to think of it as a timer on a bomb we were feverishly disarming, hoping we could finish before the damned thing exploded in our collective faces.

—THE LIBERTY MANIFESTO

THE DROPSHIP WOULD REJOIN THE *HYPERION* IN low Antigan orbit. Mengsk had left the surface as soon as the emitter was activated, but he didn't want to try to run the Confederate blockade above without gathering all his wandering, barefoot children home. At least that's how it seemed to Mike.

As they rose from the surface, Mike watched the screens. All the ship's cameras were directed toward the surface. The emitter was already having an effect on the Zergs below. They were boiling out of their nests like angry ants, moving randomly, even attacking each other in psionic-inspired madness. But soon they started descending on the tower where Mike and Kerrigan had left the emitter. A hurricane of living creatures circled the beacon like moths around a flame.

As the ship rose higher, its sensors picked up other nests, other reactions as the ever-sounding chord that came from Kerrigan's mind echoed and reverberated, growing stronger by the second. There were radioed cries from Confederate ground troops as they were overwhelmed, and the night side of Antiga Prime was now dotted with small explosions. The rebels had more warning, but those who were too slow to get off the ground were swallowed in the waves of zerglings and hydralisks.

The dropship continued to rise, and Mike could see the curve of the horizon. There was a bright flash along it, and a few seconds later the electromagnetic pulse swept over the ship. The screens went momentarily blank before countermeasures kicked in. One of the great *Behemoth*-class cruisers, sister ship to the

Norad II, had gone down beneath the growing assault.

Above them the Confederate blockade was already disintegrating. Available ships with landing capability were being rerouted, while others were trying to strafe the now ever-present Zerg.

There was a triad of glowing triangles that streaked near them, and Mike blinked as they left hot patterns on his retinas. The Protoss were already present—not in force, but still in the atmosphere.

Then came reports from the ships farthest out. Warps were opening in space, and through the warps were coming hordes of Zerg. The lobster-brain-jellyfish, the queens, the mutalisks, and the strange flying crabs were all erupting from space and descending on Antiga, summoned forth and trapped by its siren call.

The dropship docked with the larger *Hyperion*, and the entire crew evacuated the smaller ship. The dropship itself was abandoned, jettisoned from the lock, and left to go spinning down toward the surface. Its presence would only slow the *Hyperion* from its escape, and there was no time to secure it.

Mengsk's ship rose like a bubble among the panicked Confederates and descending Zerg. The Zerg fought only when there was something in their way, and the Confederates did not disappoint, putting their best ships in the path of the assault. There were several more flashes, but the *Hyperion* showed the explosions as only slightest flickers, each brief dimming representing the deaths of five hundred more Confederate humans in a nuclear fireball.

Kerrigan was worn and white-faced. Mike was sure she could still hear the psionic call, even at this altitude. It worked on some level that he could not be sure of, and pulled across the depths of space to bring in the enemy. He helped her out of the landing bay.

Raynor came across them in a gangway. "Congratulations, you two," he said warmly. "You really lit a fire under the Zerg's backsides. I don't know what you said, Lieutenant, but it sure brought them running."

Kerrigan's head came up, her eyes blazing with fury, and even Raynor could see the rage and frustration behind them. Then, as suddenly as it appeared, it was gone, expended, leaving only exhaustion in its wake.

Raynor reached up to touch Kerrigan's shoulder. His voice softened, and his forehead creased in concern. "Lieutenant, are you all right?" He separated the words with slight pauses, Mike noted.

Kerrigan looked up again into Raynor's eyes, and there was no anger there. Mike thought of the feedback loop—fear breeding fear, concern breeding concern. "I'm fine," she said, pushing a stray strand of red hair out of her face. "It's just been very tiring."

Mike said, "Mengsk?"

"Up in his observation dome," said Raynor. "I think he wants to watch the battle. I left him to it. Nothing I really want to see."

"I can report to him, if you want to rest," Mike said to Kerrigan.

She paused for a moment, and almost physically wavered. "If you would, Michael," she said. She was still looking at Raynor.

"You look really beat," said Raynor to the lieutenant, his concern so obvious that even Mike could read it. "You want to grab a cuppa joe in the galley? Maybe talk?"

"Coffee would be nice," said Kerrigan, and a small smile tugged at the corners of her mouth. "Talk too. Yes. Talk would be good."

Mike held up a hand and headed for the lift, leaving the pair in the hallway. As he hit the lift doors, he put one thought at the top of his mind, where Kerrigan could easily find it.

Remember to let him finish his damned sentences, he thought, and then rose to find the architect of Antiga Prime's destruction.

Mengsk was alone on the observation deck, his hands behind his back, facing the main screen. The chess set had been set up for a new game, and a fresh pack of cigarettes sat next to the ashtray. Two brandy snifters and a still-corked bottle of cognac rested on the bar.

All the screens but the main one had been turned off, and the last screen showed a real-time display of Antiga Prime, hovering at the center. Small yellow triangles represented Confederate forces, red triangles the ever-multiplying Zerg. A few blue-white pips that Mike had never seen before were on the surface. There were also a few circles planetside: rebel forces that had been unfortunate not to have escaped in time. As Mike watched, they were subsumed in a wave of red triangles.

It was a similar story in orbit. More red triangles, each representing tens or hundreds of Zerg fliers, all converging on Antiga Prime. The ships that bolted were untouched. Enough stood and fought to form clustering points as the Zerg swarmed over them, ripping them apart in space.

Mike remembered the image of the *Norad II* going down. This was a hundred times worse.

"We're pulling away at top speed," Mengsk said reassuringly. "I have the ship's computer compensating to keep the scale the same."

Mike crossed to the bar, pulled the cork, and poured himself an inch of cognac. He did not pour any for Mengsk.

"We calculate that, based on the strength of the emissions, we are calling every possible Zerg from twenty-five light-years out to us," continued Mengsk. "Maybe more. Lieutenant Kerrigan is quite the siren, luring these sailors to their doom."

"It took a lot out of her," Mike said, taking a long pull on his snifter.

"But not more than she could handle. I am glad you were there for her. She might not have made it, otherwise."

Mike felt his face flush, and for a moment thought it only the brandy. "You didn't leave me much choice, did you?"

"Not really." Mengsk shrugged sheepishly and turned toward Mike. Behind him, the red triangles multiplied. There was almost nothing left of the Confederate forces on the ground. "But I'm still glad you were there for her."

Mike snorted and took another drink. Mengsk poured himself one. Blue-white triangles were appearing now at the edge of the screen. The Protoss had arrived in force.

Mengsk looked at the screen and said, "Interesting report while you were gone." Mike said nothing, and Mengsk continued, "Protoss ground forces pitched in to engage the Zerg we encountered. Their leader's name is Tassadar. He calls himself the High Templar and Executor of the Protoss Fleet. His flagship's name is the *Gantrithor*."

"Maybe they were impressed with your work and decided to lend a hand. You must have a good press agent."

Mengsk gave Mike a withering look. "Come now, Michael. I expect better from you. Work out what I just said."

Mike was silent for a moment, then said, "Ground forces?"

Mengsk brightened. "Exactly. Individual warriors in very ductile power suits. Strange bug-like vehicles. Spell-casters that I can only assume are psionicists of some type. Tougher than the Zerg, man for man, though the Zerg have it all over them in raw numbers. Very intriguing, watching them battle. You might want to review the tapes later."

"Hang on," said Mike.

Mengsk's smile broadened. "I'll wait. You'll get it. I believe in you."

"If the Protoss have ground forces . . ."

"Quite good ones, I think I just said."

"That means they've fought the Zerg on the ground before. And more important, they've won those battles."

"Or why maintain a ground force in the first place? Yes! Take it to the last step."

Mike's eyes opened wide. "Which means the Zerg can be destroyed without blowing up the planet they're on!"

"Full marks!" Mengsk took a sip from his snifter. "It may be a difficult task, and I think that the Protoss are overmatched in this case, but yes, the Zerg can be beaten on the ground." He chuckled. "I had to explain it to Raynor three times, you know."

"But," said Mike. "But then all we've done is to just set the Protoss up to blow up Antiga Prime!"

"And a large piece of the Zerg forces with it. It should rock them back on their heels for a while. Long enough to let us get the upper hand against the Confederacy."

"They'll blow up Antiga Prime, and with it any surviving humans!"

"No humans would survive that many Zerg. We will do whatever it takes to save the greater humanity," Mengsk said solemnly.

"Even if we have to kill all the humans in order to do it," Mike snapped. Mengsk said nothing, and Mike just let the silence expand to fill the dome. On the main screen, Antiga was nearly covered with red triangles, and a perimeter of blue triangles was in orbit around it. There were no yellow triangles left.

After a moment, Mengsk said, "I know what you're thinking."

Mike set his glass down. "You're a telepath, too, now?"

"I'm a politician, as you're wont to tell me. And that means that I'm sensitive to other people. Their needs, their desires, their motivations."

"So what am I thinking?" Mike suddenly felt like a bug under a microscope.

"You're asking yourself if I would sacrifice you for the good of all humanity. The answer is yes, in a heartbeat and without remorse, but I really don't want to. Good help is, as they say, hard to find. And you're very good, at more than just being a reporter."

Mike shook his head. "How do you do it?"

"Do it?" Mengsk canted his head.

"Find everybody's button and press it. You play people like they were pianos. Kerrigan would leap into a hydralisk's mouth for you, Raynor will jump through hoops for you, hell, you've even gotten that old pin-headed gorilla Duke eating out of your hand. Doesn't that bother you?"

"No. It's a gift. I find that others tend to be scattered in their thinking. I try to provide a strong center for them. Raynor is in many ways consumed by anger for the Confederates: I am but a means by which he can vent that anger. Duke looks for nothing more than political cover to let him settle old scores and create new atrocities: I provide that. Sarah? Well, Lieutenant Kerrigan has always sought approval, despite her own gifts. I provide that as well."

Mike thought of Sarah Kerrigan, down in the galley, talking with Jim Raynor over coffee. He asked, "And me?"

Mengsk gave a great smile and shook his head. "You want to save souls, dear boy. You want to make a difference. Whether you're covering some traffic tie-up or rooting out some alderman's corruption, you're trying to make things better. It's practically in your genetic code. And you believe in it. *That* makes you very valuable. It makes you an incredible resource. You keep Raynor from being too impulsive, Kerrigan from being too inhuman. They both respect you, you know. You wrote off General Duke as hopeless, I think, soon after you met him, but I do believe you still hold out hope for me. That's why you've hung around, in hopes that I will find my own redemption."

Mike frowned. "And what keeps me from leaving now, knowing that this hope for your salvation is probably misplaced?"

"Ah," said Mengsk, watching the screen. The Protoss encirclement was almost complete. "Part of it is your concern for others. But I can be honest with you, now, because the Confederacy, through its puppet the UNN, has betrayed you. It has used your face and words against you. Now you've got your own personal reason to fight them. Your own reason to commit. They have made it *personal*. You can go on your own . . ." Mengsk let his voice trail off.

"But where would I go," Mike said in a flat tone. A statement, not a question.

"Exactly. You're in for the long haul. Until victory or defeat. Ah, it begins. Will you watch with me?"

Mike looked at the screen, at the ring of blue-white triangles surrounding the doomed world. Already spearheads of red were rising from the surface, but they were repelled as the Protoss built up their weapons charge to burn the world, to sterilize it to the deepest tunnels.

"I'll pass," said Mike, his mouth like ashes. He turned and walked toward the lift, not turning back to watch.

Mengsk did not seem to notice Mike's departure. He stood, snifter in hand, and watched as the Protoss rained poisonous flame onto Antiga Prime.

CHAPTER 14

GROUND ZERO

The use of the psi emitter on Antiga Prime was a watershed event, a Rubicon, a point of no return. It was like the first appearance of ghosts in the Confederacy ranks, or the indiscriminate use of the Apocalypse bombs that leveled Korhal IV. It changed everything.

It also changed nothing. For the average citizen caught between the rebels and the Confederates, and the Confederates caught between the Zerg and the Protoss, the war was still as deadly as ever. More planets would vaporize under the Protoss's weapons, and more humans would be swallowed by the Zerg hives. Yet after the swarming of Antiga Prime, there was renewed hope among the rebels. Now, at least, we had a weapon.

And like the damn-fool humans we were, we could not resist using it.

— THE LIBERTY MANIFESTO

TEN DAYS LATER, THEY WERE ON TARSONIS ITSELF, blockbusting through the densest of the downtown districts.

The city had taken the assault hard. The western precincts were still in flames caused by a battlecruiser that had gone down in their midst, and a fountain of hot dust, laden with phosphoric heavy metals, plumed southward in the strong wind. The upper windows of most of the major buildings were shattered, and in some cases entire facades had slid from the metal skeletons beneath, leaving hills of broken glass at the titanic tower's feet.

The elegant spires of Tarsonis were nothing more than jagged, twisted remains, their fractured edges scratching the bleeding sky. The atmosphere itself was torn by the shrieks and booms of battling craft, and streaked with the smoke of downed fighters.

Most of the streets were jammed with the amorphous, burned wreckage of ground cars. Their shining paint jobs had been baked by fire and heat to a uniform gray, and the once-tinted windows were shattered, jagged holes. Initially Mike looked into the vehicles to see if he could identify those within, but after the first hour he just ignored the blackened corpses, with their burned-stick limbs and withered, screaming faces.

The only things left alive on the streets were the warriors, striving hard to kill each other.

The wreck-jammed side streets kept Raynor's unit to the main boulevards, wide streets once dominated by park-like traffic islands in the center. The trees there were toppled and burned now, and what statuary to famous Confederates remained had been amputated to mere nubs.

Raynor's unit was pinned down near one of the tri-level fountains along the central plaza. A discarded, bent brass plaque identified it as a memorial placed there by the Daughters of the Guild Wars Veterans. The fountain itself was now no more than a mound of damp debris, the only hint of its previous incarnation a stone cannon jutting from the shattered stone. Mike found himself wishing the cannon were real.

Across the plaza, past a hastily erected barricade of dead cars, an Arclite siege tank had planted itself firmly between two buildings. It sat square in their path, fully deployed, its side pontoons firmly set in the asphalt. The shock cannon sent blistering rounds overhead, and its twin 80's raked the debris of the fountain. The siege tank had become a rallying point for the Confederate Security Forces, most of them the remains of the Delta and Omega Squadrons. Now the recombined units, safe under the heavy fire of the Arclite, laid down continual suppression fire on Raynor's position.

Behind the stone cannon, Mike kept his head down and desperately slammed the side of his comm unit. It burbled frustratingly at him.

"I have *got* to think about a major career change," he muttered, then ducked instinctively as another round of fire thundered through the city's stone canyons.

Raynor slid down the debris pile toward Mike, pushing a small avalanche ahead of his heavy boots. "Any luck?" he asked.

Mike shook his head. "It's probably a general jammer unit they have in operation, as opposed to an EMP pulse that would knock out the unit. That means the radio is still working, I just can't punch through the interference. Something with more power could."

"Just freaking great. We're chewed up as it is. We can't go back, and we can't get past the tank. We need to call for an evac, but it's not going to happen if we can't get in touch with the *Hyperion*."

"You boys need a hand?" Sarah Kerrigan warped into being near them. She was dressed in her environmental suit and carried the bulky canister rifle on her back. There were dark red stains on her pants cuffs, as if she had been wading through a river of blood.

Her eyes were bright and very, very alert.

"It's good to see you, Lieutenant," said Raynor. "We were just bemoaning our fate."

"I was in the neighborhood and heard gunfire," said Kerrigan. "What's the sitch?"

"Arclite, hull down, between the buildings," said Raynor, "supported by a full squad of marines."

"That all? I thought you were having trouble."

"Anything you can do to help would be appreciated, ma'am," Raynor said, grinning.

"Piece of cake," said Kerrigan, reaching up over her shoulder and pulling the canister rifle like a sword from its sheath. "Lay down some suppression for me while I sneak up on them, will you?"

"Left or right flank?" asked Raynor.

"Left, I think," said Kerrigan, and smiled again. The

smile just accented the wildness in her eyes. "That's *your* left, Jimmy."

"You got it, Sarah," said Raynor.

Kerrigan touched a device at her belt. Her cloaking device activated and she faded from view as Raynor bellowed orders at the remainder of the squad. The gauss rifles coughed as they laid down their own devastating layer of spikes in response to the Confederate fire. Their sudden assault silenced the marines, but the Arclite's shock cannon continued to boom heavy shots over the rebels' heads.

"So you think she can do it, 'Jimmy'?" Mike asked.

James Raynor flushed and shrugged beneath his armor. "Probably. But it won't mean a damn unless we can flag a lift out of this dump."

A curtain of dueling impaler spikes flew between the two camps, and Mike wondered how Kerrigan could dance across such a battlefield. One stray shot could take out her cloak, and she would bleed under the gauss rifle's spikes like any other soldier.

Then the far flank of the Confederate flank started to collapse, accompanied by the high-pitched whine of the canister rifle. One after another the Confederate Marines twitched and fell under an unseen sniper. The flank was vulnerable, as marines started firing randomly at their suspected assailant.

There was a flicker, and Sarah Kerrigan appeared, briefly, atop the barricade of wrecked cars. She flickered out again, and the air around her was filled with spikes.

Raynor bellowed for a charge, and the remnants of the squad rose from their hiding places and ran across the plaza, their heavy boots shattering the faux granite of the walkways.

The siege tank's protective screen of Confederate marines was thrown into disarray, though the Arclite they were protecting continued to hammer the rebels' position. The 80-millimeter cannons quickly found the range of the charging rebels, while the main shock cannon brought itself around smartly, firing heavy 120-millimeter shells as it did.

Kerrigan appeared again, this time on the main deck of the siege tank, right beneath the cannon. She shoved the barrel of her canister rifle into the turret ring, then somersaulted away as the Confederate rifle fire closed in on her.

Mike imagined he could hear the rising charge of the canister rifle set to overload, and shouted out a warning. Raynor and his men needed no warning, and they dropped in place.

A red flare blossomed at the base of the tank's turret, and the blast scattered the remaining Confederates. The lesser guns were silenced, but the large shock cannon continued its traverse, firing round after round as it swung around, its programming jammed.

The shock cannon took a bite out of the corner of one of the two flanking buildings, and the ground rumbled beneath them. The cannon kept going, its barrel now glowing a dull red as it tried to swivel around, but was trapped by the structure. It continued to fire, and the great structure shook from the continued assault. The top of the tank popped open, and the crew within tried to scramble out, like clowns spilling from an overstuffed car in a circus act.

They never made it. There was a tremor that ripped through the entire plaza, and the pummeled building collapsed on the tank at its feet, tons of steel and masonry falling in on itself, raising a hot cloud of dust. Only in the quake of the building's collapse did the Arclite finally stop firing.

Raynor picked himself up off the shattered pavement, along with the remains of the squad. Mike pulled himself up as well and shouted, "Kerrigan? Lieutenant?" His voice sounded small and lost in the wake of the explosion.

Kerrigan wafted up alongside them, gray as the ghost she was supposed to be. Mike realized it was dust adhering to the cloaking field itself, forming a shell surrounding the telepath. She hit another control on her belt and turned tangible again. The lines of wear and exhaustion were now tight around her face, but her eyes were still bright. The cloak took something out of her, but she didn't want to admit it.

"Target neutralized, Captain," said Kerrigan. "But I'm afraid we can't go that way now."

"It doesn't matter," said Raynor. "The Confederates have to be regrouping by now. They should be mounting a counteroffensive soon enough. We just can't hold this area. What we need is a way to punch through the jammer."

"Jim," said Mike. "Three blocks west of here is the UNN broadcast building. Its circuits have been shielded, and it has generators in the basement. They may still have enough juice to overcome the interference."

Raynor nodded. "It might just be wreckage now, but it's worth a shot." He motioned the patrol forward. Kerrigan fell in line alongside Mike.

"So you were just in the neighborhood," Mike said to the telepath. "You just *happened* to be around?"

"I go where Arcturus Mengsk thinks I am needed most," said Sarah Kerrigan, barely hiding her amusement at Mike's thoughts.

"And what's our fabled leader up to *this* time?" Mike asked. "Jim's right. I'm getting fragmentary reports of reinforcements rolling in from the suburbs. Walkers, tanks, and bikes. It's going to get real hot here real soon. Has he got a plan for this?"

"He's told me he has."

The Universe News Network Building had fared pretty badly but was still intact. The windows along the east side were nothing more than empty holes, and one of the great letters had fallen hundreds of feet to impale itself in the twisted wreckage of the concrete beneath.

Raynor looked up at the building. "I hope the equipment you're thinking of isn't in the penthouse."

"Upper levels are for management," said Mike.

"The worker bees toil on the fourth floor. And the broadcast booth and generators are in the basement."

Though his tone was glib, his heart sank. This had been his base of operations for years, his home away from home. He had grabbed a dog and soda where the huge "N" now rested, arguing planetary politics and local ordinances with the copywriters and stringers. There had been a pretzel stand next to the honor boxes. Now there were just twisted reinforcement bars jutting out of the concrete, and no sign of survivors.

The patrol moved inside. Mike didn't expect any inhabitants, but the ghostly stillness covered the lobby like a shroud. Even on weekends there was a continual hubbub here. Now there were only scattered paper and asbestos dust shaken loose from the ceiling tiles.

It was quiet, save for the crunch of their own boots. Mike glanced up the broad stairs to the mezzanine and arcade levels (quicker than the elevators even when the lifts were running), and thought about finding his old desk. Wondered if his stuff was still there.

He wondered if there was anything there he really needed.

Raynor caught him looking up. "I thought you said the equipment was downstairs."

"Yeah, just dealing with my own ghosts," said Mike, a grim tenor in his voice. He led the squad through the debris, downward, into the building's primary basement.

Whatever else Mike thought of management, they were green-tag former military, and that meant they thought in terms of triple redundancy. The main power had been cut, but the broadcast studio was packing its own batteries, and if need be, old gasoline generators for power. The link to the tower was still solid, despite all the fighting, and UNN kept underground lines to various outposts through the globe-girdling metropolis. Many of these had been cut, and their red telltales winked evilly on the primary board.

Even the air conditioning was still working, and their visors frosted at the sudden temperature change.

Raynor looked around uncomfortably. It was too easy for a stray shot from the outside chaos to bring the building down on top of them, to make this their tomb. To Mike he said, "This going to take long?"

Mike shook his head as he ran leads from the field comm unit into the main board. "Just need to boost the signal. Piece of cake. Here we go." He flipped a toggle and said, "Raynor's Rangers to Mother Ship. Do you read? Rangers to Mother Ship. *Hyperion*, you there?"

The speakers crackled and spat, and a balding female face appeared on the miniscreen. "Mother Ship. Crap, Liberty, you almost blew out my eardrums. What are you broadcasting on?" The voice was vaguely familiar.

"Old UNN surplus. Power of the press," said Mike. "We're at the Network offices. Unit's pretty shot up, and the uglies are regrouping. Need an evac."

"Working," said the voice on the other end, and Mike placed it. The tech from the bridge of the *Norad II*. One of Duke's people. "There's a park four blocks south of you. Can you pull back that far?"

Mike looked at Raynor and Kerrigan. Both nodded. "Affirmative," he said. "See you there, thirty minutes ETA."

"Roger that," said the tech. "Hold on. Patching you through to headquarters."

Mike's brow furrowed at the delay, then Mengsk's graying face materialized on the screen. "Michael," he said, his voice grim, and Mike noticed lines of concern at the corners of his eyes. "Are Kerrigan and Raynor there?"

"Still with you," said Raynor. "The lieutenant's here as well."

"Excellent, report when you get back." Something beeped to the terrorist's right and he reached over. General Duke appeared on another screen.

"This is Duke." He looked more than ever like a foul-tempered gorilla. "The emitters are secured and on-line. Returning to the command ship."

"Emitters?" Mike asked. "Psi emitters?"

Kerrigan leaned on the console over Mike's shoulder, her face close to the screen. "Who authorized the use of psi emitters?"

Mengsk's face grew stony. "I did, Lieutenant."

"You going to bring the Zerg here? Siccing them on the Confederates on Antiga was bad enough. This is insane!"

Raynor broke in as well. "She's right, man. Think this through."

Mengsk let out an angry exhalation. "I have thought it through, believe me." He paused and watched the three of them through the network feed cameras. On another screen, General Duke looked like the cat that swallowed the canary. "You all have your orders. Carry them out."

Then the screen went dead.

"He's lost it," said Raynor. "He's gone over the edge."

Kerrigan shook her head. "No. He has to have a plan."

Raynor said firmly, "Yeah, he has a plan. He plans to let the Protoss and the Zerg burn up the Confederacy one planet at a time, and take over what's left."

Kerrigan shook her head again. "He's always had a way to take care of things. He's not afraid to sacrifice, but he's no fool."

"He's not afraid to sacrifice," said Raynor grimly. "Confederates. Zerg. Protoss. When is it going to be our turn?"

"I'll talk to him when we get back," said Kerrigan.

Mike sat there, staring at the now-dead screen. "He's a politician," he said. "He weighs every decision on how far it advances him on his personal path to power. Never forget that."

Raynor opened his mouth to say something, but there was the sound of rifle fire above.

"Visitors," said Kerrigan.

"We've been rumbled," said Raynor. "Probably they caught some of the signal we pushed out. Let's go."

"Right. One more thing," said Mike, pushing himself away from the console and heading deeper into the basement.

"Liberty?" said Raynor. "What the hell?"

"He's after something else," said Kerrigan. "I'll go after him. You take care of the visitors. I read only a handful of marines. You can handle it. Watch out, one's a firebat." And she was gone as well.

She tracked Mike to another staircase, this one spiraling into the dimly lit darkness below. Pumping her canister rifle, she carefully climbed down after him.

Mike was in front of a steel door, bashing at the padlock with the butt of his gun.

"We should go," said Kerrigan.

"In a moment. This is Handy Anderson's secret stash. His secrets. I hadn't thought about it until just now. No one was usually allowed down here. It's supposed to be the records backup, the records morgue, but it's also where Anderson kept his dirt on everybody in the city."

"It's data you can use," said Kerrigan calmly, picking up Mike's surface thoughts. "You can look through it and see if there were any warnings, anything that was kept hidden, about the Zerg and the Protoss. Stuff that might have made a difference, if only people had known about it."

"Hindsight is twenty-twenty," said Mike.

"Stand aside," said the ghost. The canister rifle whined under a charge, and she fired a bolt into the lock. Fragments of metal flew in all directions.

The cache, no bigger than a broom closet, was lined with thin shelves. There were boxes of disks on all the shelves.

"We can't take it all," said Kerrigan.

"Take as much as you can." Mike opened his own pack and pulled out supplies and spare ammo, replacing them with the disks. "If Mengsk is really going to kill this planet, I want some of our reports to survive. And maybe we can figure out what really happened here."

Kerrigan opened her own pack and started shoving disks in as well. They would still have to leave the bulk of it behind.

"Don't sweat the earlier stuff," said Mike.

"You think Mengsk is really serious about the psi emitters?" Kerrigan asked, getting Mike's answer as soon as she asked.

Mike spoke anyway. "Like I said, he's a politician. If he can force the Confederates to back down with a threat of the emitters, he'll do it. If he doesn't, well, Tarsonis is one more casualty in his war. He can justify it. Someone on Tarsonis gave the order to kill his homeworld."

"But this is the heart of the human worlds. The biggest and the brightest. The center of humanity."

"This is Mengsk. With the psi emitters, he's bigger than worlds."

"I can't believe he'd do this. I've read his thoughts, like yours and Jim's. He wouldn't do this."

"You said yourself that when you're with him, he believes in every word he says, deep in his heart."

"Yeah."

"Then, next time you're with him, look deeper. There. That's as much as we can take. What's the story topside?"

Kerrigan said nothing, and Mike wondered if she was thinking about his question or his earlier suggestion. Finally she said, "They're fine. More Confederates on the way. Let's go."

Mike pulled up his pack and started out of the room. "Think about what I said, okay?"

"Thinking," said Kerrigan with a grim smile, "is the one thing a telepath *can't* avoid."

CHAPTER 15

THINGS FALL APART (IT'S SCIENTIFIC)

Everyone hates surprises. In the final days of Tarsonis, sur-
prises were the nature of the campaign. Units appeared
where none had been reported, secret transmissions threaded
between allies, battle plans were activated that we had no
idea were in place. We found out how many moves out those
plans had been laid. In a word, we had been foxed.

But even those in charge got their own surprises. As any
operation gets larger and larger, more pieces slip between the
fingers, more pieces are ignored, until things start happening
that you have no idea were about to occur. That's what hap-
pened to Mengsk at the end, when suddenly some of his loyal
soldiers had second thoughts and the chess pieces weren't
moving around the board the way he wanted them to.

And that's probably why he kicked the board over.
Heckuvan end-game strategy, but it works.

Supposedly if you are in control of everything, you hate
surprises. But I'll tell you, when you are not in control, you
hate them even more.

—THE LIBERTY MANIFESTO

THE DROPSHIP MET THEM IN ATKIN'S SQUARE. AS the remains of Raynor's team boarded, a group of techs in lightweight armor disembarked. With them was one of Duke's ghosts, the telepath's face hidden behind an opaque visor.

"This ain't no place for soft targets," said Raynor. "You boys don't even have decent armor."

"Yeah, but we got orders," snarled the captain in charge, and they pushed through Raynor's men and out into the city, heading in the direction from which the rangers had come.

Mike supposed that Mengsk had figured out there were things to loot from the UNN building. He suddenly felt very good about the backpack full of stolen secrets he had brought with him. Something he could use as leverage with the rebel leader.

Then he looked at Kerrigan. Kerrigan was looking at Duke's ghost. The blood had drained from her face.

"What's wrong?" Mike asked.

Kerrigan just shook her head and said, "We'd better get back to the command ship."

As soon as they returned to the *Hyperion*, Raynor was summoned into General Duke's wardroom to discuss strategy, "at his soonest convenience," as the message said. Muttering a string of obscenities, the former marshal lumbered forward, not even shucking his battle armor. Mike popped his own visor and seals and climbed out of the suit. Kerrigan, stripping her lighter armor with practiced ease, was already heading for the exit.

"Hang on," said the reporter. "The *Uber*-Mengsk wanted both of us to report in when we got back. I'll go with you."

Kerrigan said, "Let me talk to Arcturus on my own. He'll be more forthcoming with me." She strode down the halls of the *Hyperion* toward the lift to his observation post.

Mike considered going after Kerrigan, but she was right. The rebel leader and the ghost had a history, and Mengsk would be more willing to open up to her.

And maybe, Mike thought, she'd be able to pull something useful out the terrorist's mind. Like what he was thinking in planting more psi emitters.

Mike looked around. Most of the rest of the unit had stripped and were heading for the showers. Raynor himself would be with the general in the wardroom. Not that the general would be the best company right now, but talking to him beat cooling his heels until Mengsk rang him up.

And he didn't want to be caught stuck in the shower if Kerrigan needed him.

As Mike moved through the ship, he thought about the tech he had spoken with over the comm unit. Now that he noticed, most of the crew on the *Hyperion* were strangers: members of the Alpha Squadron as opposed to Mengsk's original rebels from before Antiga Prime. One by one, those original revolutionaries had fallen by the wayside or been promoted to other ships. Part of a plan by Mengsk to spread his agents among all the ships of his fleet, or part of a plan by Mengsk to move the old guard aside in favor of professional soldiers?

Whichever it was, Mike was sure that it was part of a plan by Mengsk.

Mike was almost to the wardroom when the door exploded, and two men in combat armor tumbled out.

It was Raynor and Duke, locked in each other's arms. The former lawman had already ripped off the shoulder plate of the general's suit and spiderwebbed the man's visor with a steel-shod fist. Duke was no slouch, however, and there were several new dents in Raynor's already-rumpled chest plate.

"Jim!" shouted Mike. Despite himself, Raynor turned toward the reporter.

General Duke did not miss the opportunity, slamming both fists into the side of Raynor's helmet. The former marshal staggered back a step, but did not fall.

Now free of his opponent's neosteel embrace, Duke went for his side arm, a nasty needle-gun that could penetrate bulkheads. Raynor recovered as the general brought the weapon up and grabbed the older man by the wrist. Then, the servos in both sets of armor squealing, Raynor slammed Duke's arm against the bulkhead.

Once. Twice. On the third time something cracked in Duke's gauntlet and the general screamed. He dropped the gun and sank to the deck. The needler went skittering across the floor. Mike knelt down, grabbed it, and rose, clamping it to his own belt for safekeeping.

Only then did Mike become aware that they were not alone in the hallway. Ahead and behind them were armed marines, their weapons leveled on Raynor and himself.

"Y'all just signed your own death warrant, boy!" Duke snarled. There was blood at the corner of his mouth, and he cradled his pistol hand. More than metal had been shattered by Raynor's blows.

"You just signed the death warrant of your home planet, General!" Mike snapped. To the marines he said, "He just set off the emitters. He called the Zerg here! Dammit! He and Mengsk didn't even give the Confederates a chance to surrender! The Zerg are coming here, and this bastard is the one who rolled out the welcome mat!"

Some of the marines lowered their weapons. They seemed suddenly to be having second thoughts about the revolution, or were suddenly worried that the Zerg were going to show up on their doorstep. Others kept a flinty-eyed, neutral glare, and their weapons remained aimed at Raynor's chest.

Mike figured the ones who were hesitating were the ones who weren't neurally resocialized. The others were waiting for the kill order.

"I'll have you court-martialed!" said the general. Mike let out a thin breath. Duke was threatening, not ordering Raynor's death. He was concerned that Mengsk might not approve.

"You want my rank, you can have it," Raynor said hotly. "And I'm not in your chain of command. I answer to Mengsk, same as you. You can't do squat without Mengsk's say-so."

"And whose orders do you think I was following when I activated the emitters, boy?" said Duke, smiling despite his pain.

"You set off a dozen emitters on Tarsonis!" said Raynor. "The populace will be swarmed!"

"We set them off in strong Confederate locations," said Duke, "and evacuated most of our regular troops. Hell, boy, didn't you realize that we were planting one more when we picked *you* up?"

Mike suddenly thought of the ghost and the tech crew, and the way Kerrigan had reacted. Of course Mengsk wouldn't care about information. He was after control of the entire realm of human space.

Raynor spat. "You son of a . . ." He took two steps toward the general.

General Duke, in his armored battle suit, held up his good arm. Not to attack, but to ward off a blow. The general was afraid, an old man quailing in a neosteel shell.

Raynor paused for a moment, then spat again. He wheeled and headed for the lift to the observation dome.

None of the marines in the hall stopped him. Some didn't have the guts to open fire on one of their own. Some didn't have the orders. And some didn't know which man was the true criminal.

Mike followed Raynor. Behind them General Duke bellowed for the soldiers to get back to their stations.

Mike laid a hand on Raynor's shoulder, and the big man turned. For a moment Mike was afraid that Raynor was going to take a swing at him, but the fire in the man's eyes was replaced with deep, bitter sadness.

"They didn't even give them a chance," he said. "They could have used it as a threat, but they just set them off. No warning, nothing. While we were en route back to the ship. They set them off."

"So what are you going to do?" Mike asked.

"I'm going to have it out with Mengsk himself," said Raynor. "He's got to be made to see reason."

"You're not going up there. Right now Duke is probably on the blower with him, calling for your hide. You've got about ten minutes before he convinces some of his followers to arrest you. With or without Mengsk's permission."

"Yeah," Raynor said bitterly. "And the way I feel right now, I'd probably take a shot at Mengsk as well."

"Well, there's that. And Mengsk *will* have you killed if you do that."

"So your prescription is, Doctor Liberty?" said Raynor.

"Go find some allies. The rest of your unit from planetside. Any of the old colonial militia from the Sara system, if any of them are left on board. Go there and stay there until I call for you. And here." He passed the pack to him. "Hold onto these. There's juicy gossip on those disks."

"Where are you going?" Raynor asked.

"*I'm* going up to the observation deck. I need to talk to the great man himself. I'll try not to hit him."

Raynor nodded and stomped off, the bag of secrets looking small and insignificant in his heavy hand. Mike took a deep breath, closed his eyes, and repeated the mantra.

"I am *not* going to hit him," he said softly. "I am *not* going to hit him."

The doors to the lift opened, and Kerrigan stalked out. Her face was a roiling storm cloud of anger and doubt.

Mike jumped back as if she had been General Duke swinging an armored fist.

"Lieutenant," he said. "Sarah, what's wrong?"

"I spoke with Arcturus," said Kerrigan, and for the first time that Mike could remember, she stammered, unsure of how to phrase her next words. "He . . . he explained himself. And his explanation was full of examples and buzzwords and quotes and omelets and breaking eggs and freedom and duty and everything else. And he had me believing, Mike. I really wanted to believe that he had information we didn't, like there were Zerg queens in the heart of Tarsonis itself, calling the shots through puppet rulers, sacrificing the populace, and eating babies in the streets."

She took a deep breath. "But as I listened, I watched the map of Tarsonis on the planet behind him."

Mike said, "I know the screen. It's his favorite toy."

Kerrigan gave a derisive snort. "As I watched, that screen turned red. All of it, red from the Zerg arriving." She looked at Mike, looking for confirmation in his eyes.

"There were no Zerg on Tarsonis until he set off the psi emitters," she said in a small voice. "None at all. It wasn't like the Sara planets, or even Antiga Prime, where there were some already there and we had already lost the world. *There was nothing there* to threaten us but other humans."

She took a deep breath and closed her eyes. "And now the Zerg are coming from everywhere. They're on the planet. Arcturus didn't recall any of the units currently in combat. He didn't even bother to get the teams that placed the psi emitters off-planet. He left them there. 'Sacrifices must be made,' he said, and he said it in that calm, pleased voice as if he were ordering coffee."

Mike thought of the team that landed at Atkin's Square, and hoped that Kerrigan was too upset to pick up his suppositions. Instead he said, "All right. He told you this. And then what happened?"

"And then word came up from the bridge about a fight between Jim and Duke." Kerrigan's face was a storm cloud again. "And he dismissed me. Just told me I had to go, just like that. And I . . . I lost my temper with him."

"There's been a lot of that going around. And for good reason."

"Mike, there was no rationale for him to do this. I

thought it was a bluff, or that Tarsonis was already infected, or that there was a master plan. It was just that Arcturus has a hammer, and when you have a hammer, every problem seems to be a nail."

Mike remembered Mengsk making the same quote earlier. It seemed like half a lifetime ago.

"It's okay," Mike said, reaching up to hold her by the shoulders. She did not turn away.

"And Mike"—her voice was a whisper—"when I got mad at him, I *looked*. I mean I really *looked* into him."

Michael waited for her to continue, but she just shook her head. When she spoke, it was in a low hiss. She spat, "That *bastard.*"

Mike said, "Look, I sent Jim down to his quarters and told him to keep his friends around him. I think you qualify."

Kerrigan looked up at Mike, and for the briefest moment she looked unsure. Then a wry smile tugged at the corners of her lips and she said, "No, I don't think so. I'm so upset right now . . . Jim would just make me feel . . ." She let out a long breath and shook her head. "I need to be alone for a little while. I need to know that I can still rely on myself. To make sure I know that I can do what needs to be done. Despite this, I'm still a good soldier, and I have a job to finish. Maybe some good will come out of this. Okay?"

Mike disagreed, but he said, "It's okay."

Kerrigan grinned. "Even if I weren't a telepath, I'd know you're lying. Mengsk is right about that. You want to save everyone from themselves. I want you to know that it's . . . appreciated."

"You watch out."

"I can take care of myself." Kerrigan managed a sure, wide-lipped smile. "I'm no one's martyr. Hell, some days I even believe that. Just tell Jim . . ." She paused and shook her head again.

"What?" Mike asked, expecting her next words.

"Nothing," she said at last. "Tell him to just watch out, too, okay? For me."

And she was gone, heading down to the dropship bays. Mike watched her stride down the hall, shedding unease and unsureness like a butterfly leaving its chrysalis behind.

Mike just wished that his stomach didn't hurt so much, and he was sure that it would be a long time before he saw her in the flesh again.

Mike took the lift up to the observation deck. Arcturus Mengsk was there, his hands behind his back, watching the screen of Tarsonis fill up with red triangles. They were nearly a blur on the screen itself, broken by the hot yellow marks of Confederate troops.

Mike noticed that the chessboard had been thrown across the room, and the pieces were scattered about. Kerrigan had definitely lost her temper.

Mengsk turned away from the map, his salt-and-pepper beard now looking more white than black. "Ah, the third of my brilliant rebels," he said. "I was wondering when you were going to turn up. Actually,

I expected you to be the first one to march in here with demands and insults, not the good lieutenant. You must have really gotten to her."

"I didn't do anything," said Mike, "but stand by her while you consigned another planet to its death."

"One death is a tragedy, a million deaths is a statistic."

"Do you keep a database of quotes to justify your excesses?" Mike asked, his eyes narrowing.

Mengsk smiled grimly. "I take it that this means you've finally given up trying to save my soul? I hope not, because after we succeed, I'll need men like you more than ever, to help form the new universal order. To help form the needed order to repel the alien menace."

"Alien menace?" Mike sputtered the words. "That would be the menace that you yourself brought down on this world? Is *that* the alien menace you mean?"

Mengsk tilted his head and pursed his brows, as if disappointed in Mike's response. Behind him, the screen continued to throb and glow, and now blue-white triangles were moving in from the edge of the screen.

What Mengsk said was, "I didn't anticipate Sarah coming up here. And I didn't expect Raynor to pick a fight with a general. That was foolish. And inconvenient. I'm going to have to smooth over some harsh feelings there."

"Harsh feelings? They nearly killed each other just now."

Mengsk shook his head again, and Mike realized that the man was minimizing the problems, just as he was minimizing the situation on Tarsonis. Minimizing them to the point where they could be ignored, glossed over, forgotten.

His own reality-warping field, thought Mike.

"General Duke is," the rebel leader said, "at heart a coward. I provide him with the spine he needs to go forward. James, on the other hand, is all courage and honor looking for a place to explode. A loaded gun looking for targets. I've given him direction. I've given him targets. Both men are very useful at what they do, and once we've taken Tarsonis, all this will wash out. Neither man can really survive without me, and to stay viable, they'll realize they will have to follow my directives."

"Are they just chess pieces to you?" Mike asked.

"Not chess pieces. Tools. Talented, useful tools. And yes. Raynor, Duke, the Zerg, the Protoss. Yes, even you and dear Lieutenant Kerrigan are all tools to achieve a greater good, a better future. Yes, things look dark right now, and I'll admit my culpability. But think of this: if things are terrible now, think how good we'll look when we take over, eh?"

"Don't look now," Mike said, looking past Mengsk, up at the screen, "but I think some more of your tools are attacking your other tools."

"Eh?" Mengsk spun in place and looked at the board. Already the first blue-white triangles, the symbols of the Protoss, were making planetfall. The red

Zerg triangles were dispersing in their wake in ripples It was as though the Protoss were stones thrown into a crimson pond.

"This is bad," Mengsk said softly. "Very bad. I did not expect them to arrive so quickly. This is very bad indeed."

"Oh my God. You *really* didn't expect this," Mike said, blinking in surprise. Then the nervousness in his stomach turned to chill fear, and he added, "Why doesn't that make me feel any better?"

CHAPTER 16

FOG OF WAR

Let's not kid ourselves, we got our heads handed to us by the Zerg and the Protoss. Yes, they were like nothing we had ever seen before. Yes, their biology was different. Yes, their technology, or what we would call their technology was more advanced than ours in dozens of areas. And of course, they were belligerent and aggressive in the extreme, they knew where we were, and they had the advantage of surprise.

But (and this is a rather large but) we humans are about the most ornery cusses in the galaxy. We had been fighting among ourselves for as long as we've been in the sector, and we had honed our own battle technologies to the point where we were their equal in many ways. We had the advantages of interior lines of supply (that's military for "surrounded") and native terrain (that's military for "we're fighting them in our living rooms"). We could have taken them if we had gotten our act together.

So what happened? The very thing that made us good warriors—the fact that we had fought among ourselves—also made us horrible at banding together in our hour of cri-

sis. We could not unite under one banner or even form a coalition. In fact, every time there was a chance for that, one faction or another did something to enhance the advancement of their own political agenda over the other factions. Often at the expense of the rest of humanity. I can't imagine the hive-minded Zerg or the glowing Protoss falling prey to such basic human drives as greed and power and raw pigheadedness.

Of course, those are all basic human drives, and that's why nonhumans were cleaning our clocks.

—The Liberty Manifesto

"YOU REALLY DIDN'T KNOW, DID YOU?" MIKE asked. "You didn't know the Protoss would get here? How could you not know?"

"Impudent pup," said Mengsk, stalking to his console and scanning a dozen screens at once. "Of *course* I knew the Protoss would get here. They follow the Zerg around like housewives chasing flies with a rolled-up newspaper, looking for them to alight so they can swat them. I just didn't expect them to get here so *soon.*"

Despite himself, Mike smiled. Anything that disturbed the great Arcturus Mengsk was enough to make him happy. And, upon consideration, if the Protoss had been in contact with Mengsk, they probably saw him for the two-faced politico he was, and they were just hanging out in warp space waiting for him to do something like this.

Mengsk cycled through a number of screens, then

cursed under his breath. Finally he opened a toggle and said, "Duke!"

The battered face of the general appeared on the screen. "Sir, have you considered my request regarding Captain Raynor?"

"Spare me your petty bickering," Mengsk snapped. "Get the local commanders on-line. The Protoss are here."

"Yes, sir, we know," Duke said proudly. "But they're avoiding our forces, concentrating primarily on the Zerg hives." He paused and blinked, completely unaware that this might be a bad thing.

"If the Protoss forces engage the Zerg," Mengsk said, enunciating each word, "then the Zerg are fighting *them* instead of the Confederates. If the Protoss engage the Zerg, the Confederates may escape. The Old Families may get away, and with them the heart of Confederate power!"

Duke blinked again, then his face fell. "We need to stop the Protoss, then. I can send them a transmission telling those glowing buzzards to back off."

Mengsk ignored him and hit some other toggles. "Send Lieutenant Kerrigan with a strike force to engage the Protoss advance party. Captain Raynor and General Duke will stay behind with the command ship."

Raynor's angry face, as red as the surface of Tarsonis, popped up on another screen. "First you sell out every person on this world to the Zerg, and now you're asking us to go up against the Protoss? You *are* losing it. *And* you're going to send Kerrigan down there with no backup?"

Mengsk's face had already changed from surprised agitation to calm reassurance. The reality bubble was disrupted, but not broken. Mike wondered how much more would be needed to bring down the entire facade the man projected. And what would happen once the mask dropped? Was there any center at all to the man to be revealed?

Mike realized he could stay, poking and arguing, and maybe even getting an angry response out of the terrorist. Mengsk was starting to look as though he might be at the end of his tether, but he was right about one thing: Michael Liberty had given up trying to save Arcturus Mengsk's soul.

And there were other, more deserving recipients of his aid.

Mike started for the lift. Behind him, Mengsk was saying calmly, "I have absolute confidence in Kerrigan's ability to hold off the Protoss."

The lift doors closed as Raynor's voice said, "This is bullsh—" And then Mike was dropping down to where, he hoped, Raynor had gathered some allies.

And despite himself, he hoped that Kerrigan had changed her mind and would be there as well.

There were about two dozen men in Raynor's barracks. Some were already strapped into their battle armor. Others were hastily suiting up. Raynor was at the comm unit.

Kerrigan was not there in body. Instead her voice, tinny over the wrist-mounted receiver, bounced upward through the room.

"But you don't owe him this!" said Raynor. "Hell, I've saved your butt plenty of—"

Kerrigan interrupted him. "Jimmy, drop the knight-in-shining-armor routine. It suits you sometimes. Just not . . ."

She paused for a moment, as if reconsidering her words. ". . . not now," she said. She sounded tired and worn. Almost defeated. "I don't need to be *rescued*. I know what I'm doing. Once we've dealt with the Protoss, we can do something about the Zerg."

She took a deep breath. "Arcturus will come around," she said, but she sounded to Mike as though she didn't hold out much hope. "I know he will."

Raynor's lips were a thin line framed by his sandy blond beard. "I hope you're right, darlin' . . . Good hunting."

He closed the link and looked up at Mike.

"We're going after her," said Mike. A flat statement of fact.

"You bet your ass we are. Suit up. Bring your gear. We may not be welcome back here afterwards."

Mike slipped into one of the empty combat suits. "Mengsk screwed up in one other place," he said, his hands now flying automatically over the fittings and seals. "Once Kerrigan engages the Protoss, they're going to treat us as hostiles. All of us. And there's a lot of Protoss hardware floating around in the system right now, orbiting Tarsonis."

Raynor grunted agreement as he ran the check systems on his own suit. He had patched up most of the damage inflicted by Duke earlier, but Mike noticed that some of the telltales were still flashing a nasty yellow warning beneath his visor.

"So we have to dodge Protoss birds as well as Zerg," said Raynor. "It's never easy around here."

"That's why we love the challenge," Mike said, more to himself than to anyone else. He hefted the knapsack of stolen data and, on the spur of the moment, shoved his old coat, the gift from the newsroom, on top. It had been singed by laser fire and spattered with blood and less recognizable fluids, and baked under foreign suns. It was tattered and ragged and bleached.

A lot like myself, Mike thought, shoving the coat down hard into the backpack, making everything fit. There was nothing else he wanted from the locker. He hoisted the sack, slung it across the back of his armor, and followed Raynor out.

The ship had gone to red alert with the first appearance of the Protoss, and now Raynor's men moved through crimson-lit hallways to the dropship bays. Mike could feel the g-forces through the deck plates; the big command ship was weaving through something, but he could not tell if it was debris or enemy fire.

"Think we can get off the ship?" Mike asked as they stepped into the landing bay.

"Yeah," said Raynor. "The dropship pilots are good

old boys. They aren't afraid of Duke's wrath, or anything else for that matter. They can always say I
threatened them into bringing us down."

"They may not be afraid of my wrath, but you
should be," said General Duke from the shadows to
one side.

The lights flashed from red to yellow, and Mike saw
Duke standing there among the dropships with two
squads of marines. They had their weapons aimed at
Raynor's men. Duke was cradling his own weapon, a
borrowed gauss rifle, in his off hand, his right hand
hanging uselessly at his side.

"Going somewhere, boy?" said Duke, a hearty
smile appearing above the sealing rim of his helmet.
There was still dried blood at the corner of his mouth.
Perhaps he thought it was a badge of honor, Mike
thought, or a slight to be avenged.

"We're going after Kerrigan," said Raynor. "She
needs backup, regardless of what Mengsk says."

"That girl needs what Mengsk *says* she needs,"
Duke drawled. "But it's nice of you to go to the effort.
Now I have solid proof of mutiny, and I can provide
the traitors to go with it."

Mike scanned the marines. They were all neurally
resocialized and, worse yet, already pumped to the
gills with stims. Their eyes were practically pupiless.
In this state they were effectively hard-wired into
Duke's nervous system. Once the general gave the
command, they would automatically jump, or fire, or
drop for twenty pushups, without thinking twice.

So the solution would be to keep the general from giving that order.

"Mengsk would be very disappointed if you killed us," Mike said.

Duke laughed. "I'll just throw one of his old quotes back at him: 'It's easier to seek forgiveness than to gain permission.' Now, you boys with Raynor, you drop the weapons now and surrender. I might even let you live if you do."

Raynor didn't move. Behind him, Mike could hear some of their rangers slowly laying their rifles on the deck.

Then the *Hyperion* pitched to one side, hard. Something big had slammed into its side. The marines, in their bottom-heavy boots, rocked in position, and Duke's aim was thrown off for a moment.

When he could bring his weapon back around, Raynor had his own rifle unslung and ready.

"This just gets better and better," Duke said, smiling through yellowed, peg-like teeth.

"I don't think you have the guts," said Raynor.

"You so much as blink, boy, and my men will fill you with so much metal you can run a scrap drive. Now drop your weapon by three. One . . . Two . . ."

There was a high-pitched whine, and Duke's left shoulder exploded in a shower of molten metal. Duke's marines all jumped and brought their weapons around, but did not fire. They had been ordered to wait for the command.

The general slowly dropped to his knees, his own

weapon clattering to the ground. His armor hissed as locking rings isolated the wounded shoulder and medpacks pumped narcotics into the general's bloodstream.

Smoke curled from the barrel of the needle-gun. Mike thumbed the hammer of the weapon back, and another round clicked into place.

"I think it's time you just shut up," Mike said to the general.

"I can have you burned where you stand," said Duke. The meds in the armor were already taking effect, and his voice was slurred.

Mike took two steps forward and said, "Go ahead. You'll go first. Give the order, General."

Duke hesitated, his eyes unfocusing for a moment as the drugs hit his system hard. He was striving to stay awake on sheer cussedness.

"You don't have the guts," he managed.

"Try me," said Mike. "I've finally learned to shoot a human target."

There was silence in the landing bay for a moment, then Raynor said, "Men, pick up your weapons. We're moving out."

Raynor's men picked up their guns and threaded their way through the rebel marines. Without Duke's specific orders, they would not fire on possibly friendly targets. Raynor paused by Mike and the kneeling Duke.

"Go ahead," said Mike. "I'll catch up."

Duke's face was ashen, and his eyes were milky

and pupilless. No rational thought was left, only hatred and cowardice warring in his mind. He hissed, "If I ever see you again, I'll kill you."

"Then get a good look at my back," said Mike, "because that's the only way you'll get a shot off in time."

Then the drugs took full control and Duke pitched backward.

Mike turned to the zombie-faced marines. "Get him to sickbay pronto, and clear the bay for liftoff." The marines managed a grunt and left, taking their fallen leader with them.

Mike ran for the dropship. The engines were already starting to whine as he charged up the gangplank.

Raynor had been right about the dropship pilots. The pilot had the coordinates punched in and clearances made before Mike had gotten on board. Now the atmosphere was evacuated and the dropship pitched out of the *Hyperion* and into the chaos beyond.

Space was being ripped apart all around them. The *Hyperion* was flying through a debris field, pieces still burning as the air bled out of a pierced hull, the remains of some other human ship that had fallen in the path of the Protoss. Energy beams sliced through the vacuum, blistering the retinas of observers.

Mike slid into the nav/comm console behind the pilot's rig.

"I'm going to try to raise Kerrigan's unit," Mike said.

"She's not going to like it," Raynor said grimly, then added, "Do it anyway."

The huge carriers of the Protoss slid like great beasts through space, their attendant flocks of fighters dancing around them like golden flies. Crescent-shaped ships corkscrewed toward the planet, and needle-like fighters and scouts made of silver and gemstones lanced through the debris field.

Behind them, the *Hyperion* itself was burning in a half-dozen spots. Nothing major, but at the moment Mengsk would be worried about more than just a group of AWOL former supporters. The battlecruiser's Yamato cannon split the sky with repeated shots, breaking up units of Protoss fighters.

"We got more company!" said the dropship pilot. "Strap in and hold tight!"

Now the Zerg were rising from Tarsonis. The great flying cannons, orange with purplish wings, came aloft and splattered in the hundreds against the Protoss carriers. They were followed by the larger flying crab-things, which seemed less affected by the small fighters than the mutalisks were. As Mike watched, one of the crab-things flew into the intake of a carrier, and the entire Protoss ship went up in a ball of blue-white flame.

A pair of the winged mutalisks noticed the dropship and banked toward them, their gullets vomiting forth coiling globules of bilious matter.

The rebels had precious little in the way of defense on the dropships, and the pilot cursed and tried to bank away from the intercept course.

They weren't going to make it, Mike realized, and braced for the impact with the Zerg acid-spittle.

A trio of bolts ripped the attacking mutalisks into organic tatters, shredding their wings with laser fire. A trio of A-17 Wraiths swooped through the remains of the Zerg, and Mike caught a glimpse of Confederate insignia on the pylons of the ships. Then they were gone as well, looking for new allies and new targets.

"Any luck?" Raynor asked, leaning over Mike's shoulder.

"Lots of traffic right now," Mike snapped. "Hold on. Got a lock. She's broadcasting. I'm putting it on the screen."

"This is Kerrigan." Her face on the screen was now drawn and haggard. Frightened, Mike thought, and a cold chill ran through him. "We've neutralized the Protoss ground units, but there's a wave of Zerg advancing on this position. We need immediate evac."

Another screen winked into existence, and Mengsk's face fluttered into view. Something was sparking erratically near that face, causing him to appear and disappear like a Cheshire cat. "Belay that order," the rebel leader spat. "We're moving out."

Raynor punched the microphone button. "What? You're not just going to leave them?"

If Mengsk had heard Raynor's comment, he gave no outward sign. Given the interference, it was likely he hadn't heard. Instead he said, "All ships prepare to move away from Tarsonis on my mark."

A burst of static broke up Kerrigan's signal.

Something big had hit near her. Then she was back. "Uh, boys? How about that evac?"

"Damn you, Arcturus," Raynor said through gritted teeth. "Don't do this."

Mengsk continued to fade in and out. Finally he came in, crisp and clear. "Signal the fleet and take us out of orbit. Now!"

"Arcturus?" said Kerrigan, in comparison to Mengsk now nothing more than a ghost on the screen. "Jim? Mike? What the hell's going on up there . . . ?"

Then the fog of war swallowed her entirely, and the screens registered nothing but static.

Raynor pounded the nav/comm console in frustration.

"You break it, you bought it," said the pilot, throwing the dropship into a tight spiral to break off pursuit by a pair of crab-things. With steel nerves the pilot dropped the fleeing shuttle beneath a Protoss scout, and the crab-things set up to attack it instead.

Mike tracked the location of Kerrigan's broadcast and fed the coordinates into the helm. The ship rocked and swayed onto its new course.

Around them a hundred new stars were born and died in a matter of instants. The greatest danger now was debris from the stricken ships, and the pilot cursed a couple times as he had to lurch suddenly to avoid catching a large piece in the hull.

Finally they were in the atmosphere itself, the screens tinged orange from the reentry fires. Most of

the battle was now above them. They only had to
worry about surface units now.

But as above, so below. They were coming in low
across the rubble-strewn surface of the planet itself.
The great cities of Tarsonis were burning, the broad
plazas filled with debris and the sunward spires now
nothing more than a set of jagged, erratic teeth. The
glass of the great buildings had been completely shattered, leaving only the twisted wreckage of the steel
skeletons beneath. One great swath had been leveled
through three blocks, ending in the crippled wreckage
of a Protoss carrier, venting unearthly radiation from
every broken seam.

The buildings decreased in size as the rebels flew
toward the farmlands and suburbs, but the devastation was still severe. Mike could see craters where
ships had augured into the surface. There were
sweeping fires here as well, consuming homes and
fields, and moving among them there were warriors
from all sides.

Now there were new buildings as well along the
scorched landscape—those of the alien invaders. The
creep was everywhere, and deadly poppy-headed
structures uncoiled toward the sky. Nests surrounded
with pulsing eggs dotted the landscape.

There were other structures, too, among the debris.
These were golden, with impossible buttresses and
sweeping shells, and mirrored surfaces of unshatter-
able glass. The Protoss were setting up their defenses
on Tarsonis.

Perhaps they thought there was something here worth saving, Mike thought. That means they had more faith in humanity that Mengsk did.

The ground beneath them roiled with the Zerg, and among them, like shining knights, the Protoss warriors strode, leaving a wake of dead, oozing bodies. Four-legged mechanical spiders crawled through the ruins, and huge things that looked like armor-plated caterpillars assaulted the Zerg hives. Lance-thin fighters strafed the hulking scythe-Zergs that swept the Protoss warriors aside like a farmer threshing wheat.

Mike said, "We should be close now."

The radio scratched and spat, and a male voice, young and frightened, came on, ". . . looking for an evac. We got civilians and wounded. We can see your craft. You got room on that tub?"

Raynor was on the radio. "Lieutenant Kerrigan, are you there?"

"No Kerrigan, sir," came the crackling response. "But we're really hurting. The Zerg are everywhere, and coming in with another assault. If we don't leave now, we're not leaving." There was a tremor of fear in the voice.

Mike looked at Raynor. The large man's face was unreadable, a clay sculpture of the real thing. Finally he said, "We're going down. Tell them we're coming."

Mike nodded and said, "But Kerrigan . . ."

"I know," said Raynor, and over the background hiss of the comm unit Mike could swear he heard the sound of a heart breaking. The former lawman took a deep breath and added, "Mengsk would abandon these people like the rest. We won't. I hope that's why we're better than he is."

The dropship grounded itself at the edge of a school-turned-bunker, and refugees had begun streaming out even as the pilot hit the retros. They were led by a lanky kid who wore the tatters of a combat suit. Some volunteer from a Fringe World for Mengsk's rebellion. Mike had never seen him before.

The kid saluted Raynor and said, "Damn glad to see you. Heard the bug-out order, but no one came for us. There are Zerg all along the northern flank. Some Protoss hit them a while back, bought us a breathing spell, but I think the bugs are coming back. The creep's halfway here already, and there's nothing we can do about it."

Raynor just said, "What unit is this?"

The youngster blinked. "We're not any unit at all, sir. There are about a half-dozen units, or what's left of them, that holed up here. Confederate and rebel both, sir. When the Zerg started swarming and the Protoss started blasting, it was every human for himself."

"Have you heard anything about a Lieutenant Kerrigan?" Raynor snapped. "She was engaged in fighting the Protoss near this location."

"No, sir," said the kid. "One of the stragglers said there was a unit fighting Protoss up on the ridge." He waved in the direction of the Zerg. "If'n that's true, Zerg got 'em, I'm afraid."

Raynor took a deep breath, then said, "Get your people on the dropship. Don't worry about heavy ordnance. Leave it. It's not like the Zerg or the Protoss can use it. We lift in two minutes."

Mike came up alongside Raynor and said, "We can still search for her."

Raynor shook his head. "You heard the kid. There's more Zerg coming. With Mengsk's rebels pulling back, the entire planet's going to be awash in aliens in no time at all. The dropship has no defense, and we've got noncombatants on board. We have to get out now and hope we can bum a lift out of the system before everything goes up."

Mike put a hand on Raynor's shoulder. "I'm sorry."

"I know," said Raynor. "God help me, I know."

CHAPTER 17

ROADS NOT TAKEN

The Confederacy died with Tarsonis. So much of the power and prestige had been locked up there for so long that with its collapse the rest of the Confederacy went with it.

Arcturus Mengsk played coroner, of course, performing the autopsy and declaring that the patient had died of massive Zerg poisoning, compounded by Protoss trauma. The irony that Mengsk's fingerprints were all over the Confederacy's murder weapon mattered little to many and was ignored by most. As you might expect, it was not something UNN covered in those days.

Before the last Confederate trooper was digested in a Zerg hive, Mengsk declared the Terran Dominion in order to unite the surviving planets, a shining new phoenix that would rise from the ashes and gather together all of humanity. Only by standing together, the former rebel declared, could we come to defeat the alien menaces.

The first ruler of this bright, shining new government was Emperor Arcturus Mengsk I, ascending to the throne by popular acclamation.

The irony of this last little fact, that most of the acclamation was Mengsk's own, was also missed by most of the general populace.

—THE LIBERTY MANIFESTO

EVEN AS TIME TICKED AWAY, THEY CIRCLED FOR another twenty minutes, looking for stragglers on the ground. All they found was a lot of Zerg and a lot of land already swallowed by the creep. Finally, listening to the repeated protests of the dropship pilot, they lifted off. Beneath them, the ground churned with Zerg building new structures of gothic flesh. There were flashes of Protoss weapons crackling over the horizon like heat lightning in the summer.

Mengsk contacted the dropship on the way up, a general call to all ships within the area. The terrorist's face was calm, but it was a stone-faced calm, one that didn't project across the screen. His eyes were bright and avaricious.

"Gentlemen, you've done very well, but remember that we've still got a job to do. The seeds of a new empire have been sewn, and if we hope to reap—"

Raynor leaned forward toward the comm-mounted camera and toggled a switch. "Aw, to hell with you!" he snarled.

Mengsk heard that one. The great brow lowered between the rebel leader's eyes. "Jim, I can forgive your impulsive nature, but you're making a terrible mistake. Don't cross me, boy. Don't ever *think* to cross me. I've sacrificed too much to let this fall apart."

"You mean like you sacrificed Kerrigan?" Raynor snapped.

Mengsk recoiled as if Raynor had reached out through space and slugged him. His face reddened. "You'll regret that. You don't seem to realize my situation here. I will not be stopped."

Raynor had finally broken through the thick, deep patina that covered the leader of the rebellion and found the man beneath. Mengsk was angry now, and veins were standing out at the base of his neck. "I will *not* be stopped," he repeated, "Not by *you* or the *Confederates* or the *Protoss*, or *anyone*! I will *rule* this Sector or see it burned to ashes around me. If any of you try to get in my . . ."

Raynor hit the kill switch for the sound and watched Mengsk spit and bellow silently on the screen.

"You got under his skin," said Mike. "At last."

"Must have been something I said," Raynor said, but he didn't smile when he said it.

In the humming silence of the dropship, Mike said, "I'm sorry about Sarah." It didn't sound any better now than it had before, on the surface.

Raynor sat down next to Mike and looked at the deck for a while. "Yeah, me too," he said at last. "I shouldn't have let her go alone."

"I know what you're going through."

"What, you're a telepath now?"

Mike shrugged. "I'm a human. That's what's important. It's been a long war. We've all had losses.

We've all seen things we don't want to have seen. A smart man once told me that the living feel guilty about still being alive. And no, it's not your fault."

"Sure feels like it," said Raynor. There was a silence in the dropship cabin. Finally the ex-lawman shook his head. "It's not over," he said. "The Protoss and the Zerg aren't going to give a rat's ass that Mengsk is running things now. They don't care about human wars or human leaders. They're battling throughout humanspace. It's not over."

"I think it's over for me," said Mike, "I'm not a warrior. I've played at it, but I'm a newsman. I don't belong on the battlefield. I belong behind a keyboard or in front of a holo camera."

"The universe has changed, son. What are you planning on doing?"

It was Mike's turn to take a long pause. "I don't know," he said at last. "Something to help out, I suppose. Can't help myself there. But it has to be something other than this."

The dropship had limited range, but they managed to flag down a lift out-system on the *Thunder Child*, an old *Leviathan*-class cruiser that only four hours and one mutiny earlier had been in the service of the Confederacy. Now it and most of the human ships were pulling back out of combat, leaving Tarsonis to the Zerg, the Protoss, and whatever poor fools who thought underground bunkers were a good idea.

The comm officer of the *Child* met them at the

gangway. "I have a message for you from Arcturus Mengsk."

"Mengsk!" spat Raynor. "Is he looking for me to rip him a new orifice?"

"It's not for you, sir," said the comm officer. "It's for a Mr. Michael Liberty. Emphasis on the Mister. You can take it in the communications room, if you want."

Raynor raised a tired eyebrow. Mike waved him to come along. The former planetary marshal, former rebel captain, former revolutionary settled himself in a chair out of view of the comm console's camera. Mike toggled the reply switch and waited for the message to come through space from the *Hyperion*.

Arcturus Mengsk warped into view on the screen. Every hair was back in place, and every action mannered and rehearsed. It was as if the earlier incident had not happened.

"Michael," he beamed.

"Arcturus," said Mike, not even giving him a smile.

Mengsk looked down briefly in sorrow, as if thinking carefully about his next words. Once it would have worked, but now it was a shallow, emotionless mannerism, one that the rebel leader clearly had rehearsed. Michael almost expected him to come around and sit on the edge of the desk. "I'm afraid I can't express sufficiently my regrets about Sarah. I just don't know what to say."

"Captain Raynor had a few choice words," said Mike, his own eyes now blazing.

"And someday, I hope that Jim and I can talk about

it." Mengsk's smile was forced and strained. Something had happened, and the great bubble around Mengsk had been shattered. "But that's not why I called you. I have someone who wants to talk to you."

Mengsk reached off screen to flip a switch and a new face replaced that of the future emperor of the human universe. A balding head dominated by a pair of bushy eyebrows.

"Handy?" said Mike.

"Mickey!" said Handy Anderson. "It's good to see you, buddy! I knew that if anyone in the stable survived this mess, it would be you! You're the lucky coin, always turning up when needed!"

"Anderson, where are you?"

"Here on the *Hyperion,* of course. Arcturus had me shuttled over from a refugee ship. He's been telling me how great you've been through all this. A real trooper. Why no reports for a while?"

"I sent reports. You changed them, remember? Said Mengsk had captured me? Ring any bells?"

"A small bit of editing," said Anderson, "Just enough to make the powers that be, God rest their eternal souls, content. I knew you'd understand."

"Handy—"

"Anyway, I hear you've done a bang-up job. And I knew you'd want to know that, despite the present situation, you can have your old job back."

"My old . . ."

"Sure. I mean, the people who wanted you dead are

now no longer in the business, one way or another. I was talking with Arcturus, here, and we could make you the official press liaison to his government. He thinks the world of you, you know. Apparently you grew on him with your winning personality."

"Anderson, I don't know if . . ." Mike said, tapping his forehead with the palm of his hand.

"Just listen. Here's the deal," said the editor-in-chief. "You'd get your own office, just down the hall from Arcturus's. All access, all the time. You do the trips, cover the dinners, get the awards. Lotsa perks. Lotsa security. It's a cush job. Hell, I can get a stringer to type up your reports for you. I tell you—"

Mike thumbed the sound off. Anderson kept talking, but Mike was no longer looking at him.

He was looking at his own reflection in the smooth surface of the screen. He was leaner than when he had last been in Anderson's presence, and his hair was more rumpled. But there was something else as well. It was in his eyes.

His eyes seemed to be looking beyond the console, beyond the walls of the ship itself. It was a distant look, a hard look, a look that he once thought of as being one of despair, but now realized was determination. He was seeing a bigger picture than the one he was immediately involved with.

A look he had seen before on Jim Raynor's face, when Mar Sara died.

"How long will he go before he notices you're not listening?" Raynor grunted.

"He's never noticed before," Mike said. He sucked on his lower lip for a moment, then said, "I know what I want to do. I should start using my own hammer."

Raynor sighed. "Try that once more, in English."

"When all you have is a hammer, everything looks like a nail," quoted Mike. "I'm not a warrior. I'm a newsman. And I should start using my newsman tools for the good of humanity. Get the story out. Get the *real* story out."

Mike hooked a thumb toward the screen. Handy Anderson had finally noticed that he wasn't being heard. The balding editor-in-chief tapped the screen and mouthed an unheard question.

"I want to get as far away from Arcturus Mengsk as possible," said Mike. "And then I want to start telling the truth about all this. Because if I don't, people like *him* are going to determine what really happened." He jerked a thumb at the screen. "Him and Arcturus Mengsk. And I don't think humanity could survive those lies."

Raynor smiled, and it was a broad, earnest smile. "It's good to have you back," he said.

"Its good to be back," said Mike, looking at the far-eyed stranger reflected in the monitor. He shook his head and added, "I could *really* use a cigarette."

"So could I," said Raynor. "I don't think there are any on this tub. But look at the bright side: at least you still got your coat."

POSTBELLUM

BATHED IN LIGHT, THE MAN IN THE TATTERED coat stands in a room of shadows. The smoke from the last of a series of cigarettes snakes around him, and the ground at his luminous feet is scattered with butts that look like fallen stars.

"So what you're seeing," says Michael Liberty, the luminous figure speaking to the surrounding darkness, "is my own private little war, fought on my turf, and with my weapons. Not cruisers and space fighters and marines, but just words. And the truth. That's my specialty. That's my hammer. And I know how to use it."

The figure takes another long puff, and the final coffin nail joins the others on the floor. "And you people, whoever you are, need to hear it. True and unfiltered. That's why the holo transmissions: they're harder to fake. And I'm spreading this as far as I can, over the open wavelengths, so everyone knows about Mengsk, and the Zerg, and the Protoss. And knows about men and women like Jim Raynor and Sarah Kerrigan, so they and others like them may not be forgotten."

Michael Liberty scratches the back of his neck and says, "I went into the military thinking it was just another bureaucracy filled with craven cowards and corporate stupidity.

"Well, I was right, but I was also wrong."

He looks at the viewers with unseeing eyes. "But there are also people really trying to help others. People really trying to save others. Save their bodies. Save their minds. Save their souls."

His brow furrows, and he adds, "And we need more people like that, if we're going to survive the dark days ahead."

He shrugs again. "That's it. That's the story of the fall of the Confederacy, of the Zerg and the Protoss invasions, of the rise of Emperor Mengsk of the Terran Dominion. The battles are still being fought, planets are still dying, and most of the time, no one seems to know why. When I find that out, I'll get you that information, as well.

"I'm Michael Daniel Liberty, no longer of UNN. Now I'm a free man. And I'm done."

And with those words the figure freezes in place, trapped in its prison of light. He is caught with a tired smile on his face. A satisfied smile.

Around the hologram the lights come up, luminous bulbs that have been bred specifically for the purpose. The walls pulse and sweat, and thick, viscous fluid drips from weeping sores along that wall to keep the air moist and warm. The cable of the human-constructed hologram projector merges in a gooey lump into the organic power constructs of the main structure. The connection between the two worlds was once a colonial marine, but now serves a higher purpose for its new masters.

On semiorganic screens around the perimeter, the better brains of the Zerg discuss what they have seen. They are morphic constructs, bred only to think and direct. They too serve their higher purpose within the Zerg hive.

In the projection room a hand reaches up and touches the rewind button. The hand was once human, but is now transformed, the product of the Zerg's mutagenic capabilities. The flesh of the hand is green and dotted with chitin-like extrusions. Beneath the surface of the skin strange ichors and new organs twist and slide. Once she was human, but she has been transformed and now serves a higher purpose. She was once called Sarah, but now is known as the Queen of Blades.

The other organic minds, leaders of the Zerg, make noise in the background. Kerrigan ignores them, for they say nothing, at least nothing that matters. Instead she leans forward to study the weathered face in the holo, the face with the deep transfixing eyes. Deep within her restructured heart something stirs, a ghost of a memory of a feeling for this man. And for other men. For those who would sacrifice all for their humanity.

As opposed to merely sacrificing their humanity itself.

Kerrigan shudders for a moment as the old feeling washes over her, that now-alien feeling of her once-human nature. Yet as quickly as it appears, the emotion is suppressed, so that none of the other Zerg notice it. At least that's what Kerrigan assumes.

Kerrigan nods. She blames the reporter's words for the uncomfortable emotion. It has to be the report itself, not the memories it brings, that disturbs her. Michael Liberty always was a master of words. He could make even a queen long for her days as a simple pawn.

Still, there is much in Michael Liberty's broadcast, and much that is not realized by the nonhuman minds that are now her compatriots. There is much valuable data here. Much that can be divined from Michael Liberty's words. What he says and how he says it.

The projector chimes, signaling the rewind complete, and the inhuman hand presses the play button, then raises a finger to her very wide lips.

Kerrigan, the Queen of Blades, permits herself a small smile and concentrates on the man wrapped in light. She wants to see what else she can learn from her new enemies.

ABOUT THE AUTHOR

Jeff Grubb writes novels, designs games, and creates worlds. He lives in Seattle.

Visit
❖ Pocket Books ❖
online at

---

www.SimonSays.com

Keep up on the latest new
releases from your favorite
authors, as well as author
appearances, news, chats,
special offers and more.

SIMON & SCHUSTER
A VIACOM COMPANY
www.SimonSays.com

Pocket
Books

2381-01